S0-EIB-874

BOOKS BY

HUGH FLEETWOOD

ROMAN MAGIC 1978

THE ORDER OF DEATH 1976

A PICTURE OF INNOCENCE 1975

A CONDITIONAL SENTENCE 1974

FOREIGN AFFAIRS 1973

THE GIRL WHO PASSED FOR NORMAL 1973

A PAINTER OF FLOWERS 1972

Roman Magic

Roman Magic

HUGH FLEETWOOD

ATHENEUM
New York
1978

Library of Congress Cataloging in Publication Data

Fleetwood, Hugh.
Roman magic.

I. Title.
PZ4.F587Ro 1978 [PR6056.L38] 823'.9'14 77-12547
ISBN 0-689-10839-7

Published in England under the title
AN ARTIST AND A MAGICIAN

Copyright © 1977 by Hugh Fleetwood
All rights reserved
Manufactured by Publication Press, Inc.,
Baltimore, Maryland
First American Edition

For

George and Birgitta Cosmatos

ONE

He stood, plump and pale, on his terrace, and tried to conjure the morning into life. But perhaps because he had a slight hangover, or perhaps because it was only seven-thirty and he hadn't slept enough, or perhaps, simply, because last night's dinner party had been a disaster, the morning refused to respond. Oh sure, the white August sky shimmered intensely above him in all its early brightness, and two dark swifts who still hadn't migrated wheeled hungrily round his head. And sure, the domes of the churches quivered upwards into the quiet clear light, and the ochres and umbers of the buildings nearby were already beginning to glow. Even the flowers on his terrace, red and orange and yellow, were open and blazing at his feet, and the cat had been awake for hours. Yet though he saw all this, saw all this movement and quickness—saw the nuns on the roof of their convent pacing up and down in their black habits, with prayer books in one hand and crumbs in the other, which they dropped surreptitiously to the doves, saw the garbage men in the courtyard of his building removing the refuse of yesterday, saw bare brown arms stretching out of windows to open shutters and blinds—it was all a dull, yeastless pageant, a dough that refused to rise. He whispered to it, he sang, silently, a little song to it, he even, without moving, lifted his hand and waved an invisible wand at it. But—nothing. The spark was not there. The morning refused to budge.

He flopped down in a wicker chair and closed his eyes. Mornings like this occurred perhaps once every six months, and they crushed him when they did. For whatever philosophers might say to the contrary, he knew that only he had the power to make the world exist, to make it live. Because it was all, this world—the sky, the flowers, the domes, the doves, the colours, the nuns, the cat—within him, and what he saw were merely images projected onto an empty screen through the film of his own soul. Only the images weren't enough; he had to feel the things themselves inside him. Feel them filling him, swelling him, feeding on him and feeding him. He had, every morning, every day, every minute of his life, to create them. And this morning he couldn't. He was just looking at an old newsreel; a documentary of a world that no longer was. And oh it was all so depressing. It was worse than depressing, he told himself; it was death. Yes. That was what death was. When one no longer had the power to create the world.... But he wasn't dead yet, and he wasn't going to die for a while. He still enjoyed his creation too much. He still had so much to do. He *had* to light the fire that would set the whole business in motion for another twenty-four hours. He had to burn the old footage, and start transmitting live again. He *had* to. And what did hangovers matter, or tiredness, or even disastrous dinner parties? He was a god. He was a magician. He was—

He was a silly old fool, he muttered to himself now with a little smile, and opened his eyes. He was an overweight 58-year-old with straggly white hair who drank too much, who was sitting on his terrace in Rome feeling sorry for himself when he should be making some coffee, giving Philip-the-Cat his breakfast, showering the sweat of the night away, and going into his study to attack the mountain of scripts that should have been translated and sent back a week ago. A god! A magician! Really. *What* an old fool he was becoming.

But as he turned from the terrace and went back into the apartment, feeling quite cheerful and at peace with himself once again, he glanced over his shoulder—and saw that indeed the morning had come to life....

It had been a disastrous dinner party however, he thought, as he pottered about the kitchen surveying the remains of it, and wondering whether to clear it up himself or leave it for Aida, his cleaning woman. And that was why he hadn't slept well, and why he had a hangover—though God knows he hadn't drunk any more than usual. Even less, maybe, so intent had he been on trying to keep the peace between his various guests, and trying to give some semblance of gaiety to the evening. Not that it had been any use. He had stuffed them with food, drowned them in wine and whisky, made up ditties, put on rag-time records, told his war stories and his cat stories and his stories of the old South—had even danced for them with a tambourine, going tap on his toes and bang on his bottom and hit hit hit on his head—and all they had done was sit there, smile politely, tell him he was wonderful; and then go right back to their bickering and boringness. The ugly little Canadian lesbian had snapped at the pink and puffy portrait painter, telling him he was a snob, and the portrait painter had paid fulsome and embarrassing compliments to the old deaf princess. The old deaf princess had attacked the supercilious young writer for not being married, and the supercilious young writer had ignored her and spent the entire evening condescending to some woman from New York with a little flowered expression and a little black dress, who possibly, in other circumstances, could have been very nice, but last night had been as appetizing as a dish of cold and over-cooked rice. But then in other circumstances, by themselves or with other people, they could all be—they had all been, were—very nice. Only last night the chemistry hadn't worked.

He was, he supposed, as he decided to leave the dishes, and lit the gas under the coffee, a little too slapdash as a cook, and should take more care over the ingredients he mixed together. But that would have taken the fun out of things. And while, when disasters did happen they were dreadful, and made him feel depressed and mean, and made him regret having wasted his time and money, most evenings—and he had dinner parties almost every night—were wonderful. Or at least, he enjoyed them. Inventing all those different characters, bringing them all to life....

Though it wasn't only he who enjoyed them, he knew. Nearly everyone did. Otherwise why should they come back for more? And they came—except for the irredeemably sour, the unacceptably aggressive, the dedicatedly dull—time and time again. Both those who lived in Rome, and those who passed through in the hundreds every year. And he was sure it was just because he did mix things so recklessly—both food and people—that they came. Because no one ever knew what they'd be getting. Some great elaborate dish—or sausages and beans. Some famous opera singer or writer or surgeon—or an impoverished actor, a lacrosse coach from a girls' school in Wales, or a Danish dealer in waterbeds. Yes. That was the secret of his success—apart from the fact that he always tried to be, and nearly always was, an attentive and amusing host, whatever the particular evening's recipe—and that was why he never did take more care over his ingredients, in spite of the occasional slip-up. In fact, of all the thousands of people he knew and who came to him, all the thousands of members of this vast court of friends, acquaintances, and the merely curious, a court in which he was both the magician and the fool, only four people were not allowed to meet each other under his roof—and certainly never met each other under anyone else's. But then they were his inner court; an oligarchy of four people who adored him, hated each other, contended for his services, were jealous and sulky when obliged to remember that he didn't belong exclusively to them—and who, incidentally, supported him, when it was necessary.

Which was, alas, rather often.

Because while the translations of film-scripts that he did could feed the cat, pay the rent, and even just about cover the expense of a cleaning woman and a sweet if not over competent Irish secretary, they couldn't always pay for his dinner parties, his liquor, the odd trip abroad he took, and all the other paraphernalia that was so essential to the maintenance of his body and soul, and his particular role in the world. And so the four of them—unbeknown to the others?—sometimes helped him out. They didn't call it supporting him—they called it loaning him money. But while he had never been absolutely certain, he was fairly sure that for them the word loan was a euphemism for gift. He certainly hoped so, anyway, because he was not likely ever to be in a position to pay them back. At least not in cash. And in kind—well, he had paid them back hundreds of times over, and with interest; which was why he never felt at all guilty about applying for further loans when they were needed. He entertained them, he made them laugh; he cheered them up when they were miserable, he introduced them to the brightest and best—or the most attractive—of everyone else he knew, and above all, he brought magic into their lives. For not only could he and did he create the world afresh day by day, he also had the power—with a word, a gesture, or simply a mood—to create it afresh for other people; a power which he exercised and made available for most people only at his dinner parties, but which, for the four members of his inner court, he was willing—or obliged—to make available whenever they needed it. Most people, when they phoned during the day, were lucky to get thirty seconds of his time; a quick 'how are you', a quicker 'when am I going to see you', and that was that. But for the four he was always on tap; for ten minutes, twenty minutes, an hour if necessary. To counsel, advise, discuss, plan, distract—whatever. Not that he begrudged them his time. For one thing he was truly grateful to them for their continued support, and for another, he felt that only they truly appreciated his nature, and thought of him not as a translator of film-scripts—which was what he was forced to be—but as a poet, a novelist, a painter, an actor. An all-round artist. A magician, in other words. Which was what he was....

Quite why they hated each other so much he wasn't sure. Certainly they had nothing in common apart from their inexhaustible supplies of money and their affection for him, but to have nothing in common was hardly a reason for the animosity they felt towards each other. And animosity they felt. Pam said that Jim was depraved; Jim that Pam was evil. Betty said that Bernard was rude; Bernard that Betty was fey. Betty said that Pam was a hypocrite, Pam that—but it was a never ending circle, and all four of them, Pam, Jim, Betty and Bernard, thought that, above all, the other three were destructive forces who were preventing 'dear Wilbur' from, more than merely *being* a poet, painter, novelist and actor, actually writing poetry, writing novels, painting pictures and acting in plays. All of which, before he had come to Rome and met them, he had done. Yet though it was flattering to think this high concern for his creativity was what made them mutually detest each other, he couldn't help feeling there was more—or less—to it than that. Strangely enough, however, they had never told him, and he, who liked them all and didn't care or think it polite to press for things that weren't willingly offered, had never really asked. Also, he preferred to avoid the subject of his productivity, since it was in the name of this that he applied for and was granted his loans. Of course they all—Pam, Jim, Betty and Bernard; the four pillars of capitalism as he liked to think of them—knew perfectly well when he said 'my dear, I just have to get away for a few days to write another chapter' that write another chapter was exactly what he wouldn't do. Still, it was a pleasant fiction, a graceful way of going about something that could easily have been sordid. It had the added advantage of allowing the four to feel they were playing the part of patrons, of doing their duty towards the arts, without obliging them to take the responsibility for, or even worse, make a judgement on, the finished work. What *would* they do, he wondered, as he shuffled now out of the kitchen towards the bathroom, with a cup of coffee in his hand and Philip fed, if he actually did some major work, and they didn't like it? It would be so embarrassing. No; it was much better this way, where his art and his life were one and the same thing, and both equally products of his genius—or his talent. Besides, he sighed, as he lowered himself gently onto the black plastic toilet seat, he did produce just enough minor work every year to satisfy the vulgar minded; to satisfy those who were oblivious to his charm, blind to his originality; resistant to his magic....

The process of getting up and putting himself into gear was the slowest and stateliest of the whole day. It was also, normally, the only time of day when he allowed his mind to wander. However, it was an important time, since it set his mood for all that followed. And if he couldn't, as he nearly hadn't been able to this morning, bring the world to life, he was miserable and wretched for at least twelve hours. And he couldn't afford to be wretched for all that time. Because unless he was already in his study typing and translating away by the time Irish Lillian arrived—and stayed there till twelve-thirty, when it was generally time to make a small lunch for two or three people—the backlog of work that he just managed to keep shifting would have jammed up completely. Which would have caused a breakdown in his whole carefully balanced system. And such a breakdown would have been particularly unfortunate today, since it was the middle of August, and the Friday of the *ferragosto* holiday weekend, and almost everyone was out of town, and he was planning on doing a great deal of work. He didn't even have anyone coming for lunch! In fact, with three of the Four away, unless some very bored friend or very stray acquaintance called, with any luck he'd be able to work uninterrupted all day—or at least until three, when he took a siesta—and then again from five to seven—when he would have to start preparing dinner for those one or two people who hadn't gone on holiday. He might even, if he had a whole weekend uninterrupted, might not only be able to shift the backlog of work, but actually to clear it. Which would be a relief. Because recently things had been so tight that he'd been considering applying for a loan....

However, if he thought that he had, after a shaky start, got the day off on the right footing, and thought that he was going to get a lot of work done, he was wrong. First, because no sooner had he sat down at his desk than the telephone rang; and when he answered, an old, fluty, impervious voice said, 'Wilbur?'

It was Pam; the only one of the Four who hadn't gone away. But then it was very difficult for Pam to go anywhere. She was very old, had water on the knees, chronic asthma, and an uncertain sense of balance.

With only the slightest of silent sighs, Wilbur set his voice.

'Hello my dear, how are you?'

'Oh, not very well. I fell out of bed last night and couldn't get back in. So tiresome.'

'You should have phoned me.'

'I thought about it. But it was so late. And you couldn't have done anything. Besides,' the old voice added, with only a trace of bitterness, 'I'm quite used to sleeping on the floor.'

'Oh Pamela dear—'

'I got a letter from Bobbie yesterday.'

'How is she?'

'Oh very well. She has this new boy-friend—'

'You told me.'

'And it seems they get on splendidly. Bobbie said—'

But before Pam, whose fifty-year-old daughter was the one great passion of her life, could go on to tell Wilbur what Bobbie had said, he, thinking that perhaps Bobbie herself wouldn't be so eager to have every detail of her private life discussed over the phone, interrupted again.

'Oh, that's marvellous for her. You said he sounded very pleasant from her last letter.'

'Oh yes. He sounds very pleasant indeed. He's Hungarian. A *fish*ery expert.'

'Well I do hope they'll be happy together.'

Happiness, however, was something Pam didn't seem to be certain of. She said quickly, 'Oh I don't know about that. He's much younger than her, and as far as I can gather doesn't really have any money or prospects.'

Bobbie, Wilbur wanted to say, had quite enough for two; and besides, didn't seem the type to be interested in prospects. He had met her several times when she had come to Rome to visit her mother, and liked her very much. She did something for the Aborigines in Australia. He didn't, of course, say anything, and let Pam go flutily on.

'I should so love to go to Australia myself again sometime. To do some painting. I'm sure I'd be able to *get* some of those marvellous landscapes much better now than I did when I was young.'

'You should, my dear.'

'Do you think so?'

No, of course he didn't. For one thing, Bobbie would be furious; she relied on him to look after her mother, and discourage any of her wilder fantasies. For another, Pam, who thought of herself as a bohemian, and whose life had been dedicated to the production of minute water-colours, had *got* quite enough landscapes here. And finally—what would happen to his cover, the roof of security under which he lived, if one of the four columns that supported it were suddenly removed? He could hardly expect her to help him out from Australia. What need would she have of his encouragement and originality there?

'Yes, of course. Those colours. The space. The difference in light. It would give your paintings a whole new dimension.'

'Oh,' Pam trembled.

There was no point in *dis*couraging her though. Time would take care of this madness, he was sure.

A very short time, too; for it seemed, when next she spoke, that she had already forgotten her Australian landscapes. She said haughtily—and Wilbur guessed that this was the real point of her call—'Wilbur, could you come to tea this afternoon. I have to talk to you.'

So much for his siesta, and his working from five to seven....

'Yes of course my dear. I'd love to.'

Her point won—not that it could have been contested, and she knew it—Pam relaxed. 'The garden is so lovely now. And it's so peaceful. Everyone's away. And—could you come at four-thirty?'

'Yes of course my dear.'

'Oh good, see you then, then,' Pam said—and hung up.

What, Wilbur wondered, as he looked at the page he was working on, could she want to talk to him about? Nothing very much, presumably. Perhaps one of the neighbours' children had come into her garden to retrieve a ball, and she would want to know if he thought she should set up a mantrap to discourage further intrusions. He would, on the whole, advise against.... However, he told himself, since he *was* going to see her, and she had so upset his planned schedule, perhaps it wouldn't be such a bad idea to take this opportunity of asking her for her yearly contribution. After all—it was her turn. And while he wasn't absolutely desperate yet, it was always as well to have a little in hand, rather than wait for the actual day when one simply didn't have enough in the bank to buy a single bottle of decent red wine....

If Pam's call and invitation to tea had upset his plans for the day—which upset, however, though irritating, wouldn't be entirely without compensation—what happened next was altogether more serious, and didn't just upset his plans for the day, but destroyed them completely. And it was that when Irish Lillian arrived at ten o'clock, bringing his mail with her that she had picked up from the porter downstairs, there was, along with thank-you notes, we're-coming-to-Rome-shortly notes, wish-you-were-here cards, and a brochure from the Royal Horticultural Society of London, a large official-looking letter from the Italian Tax Department, which said that he owed the sum of six million lire for—

He couldn't go on, and sat back in his chair, feeling sick. He handed the letter to Lillian. 'Read it,' he said. 'I can't. I don't understand.'

Lillian read it and nodded, then looked up at him and smiled. She was very good natured.

'You owe the tax department six million lire.'

How soft and gentle her voice was. How infuriating.

'I can read,' he snapped. 'What does it mean? I don't understand.'

Lillian looked at the letter again. She had light brown wavy hair, pale skin and grey eyes, and was wearing a simple grey cotton shift with yellow sandals. She also wore a wedding ring on her finger though she wasn't married—she felt married, she said; to a Chinese boy—and a small gold crucifix round her neck; though she hadn't been a Catholic for years, she said. She was twenty-nine years old and—

'It's a value-added tax on all the translations you've been paid for over the last few years,' she murmured pleasantly, interrupting his attempts to calm himself by cataloguing her.

'I don't understand,' he repeated.

Nor, he guessed, did Lillian; but she made the effort he was unable to.

'All the translations you've done. You've been paid for them. When you charged for them you were supposed to add a percentage that you were then meant to pass on to the tax people. It's a value-added tax,' she said again.

'But I've always paid taxes,' Wilbur wailed. 'Here, in America, in England. Everywhere I've ever published a book, or made a film, or had an exhibition. In France, Germany, Yugoslavia, Spain, Portugal, New Zealand, Australia, Japan, Egypt, Switzerland.' His mind reeled as he paused for breath, and tried to remember all the other countries in the world. 'Luxembourg, Brazil, Argentina—Ireland,' he gasped, in case Lillian should feel left out or offended. 'Belgium, Holland, Denmark, Sweden—' he stopped, realizing he was getting hysterical. 'Get me a brandy,' he ordered.

Lillian did, and he felt ashamed of himself for being so rude.

'Have one yourself, dear child.'

Lillian smiled, and said no.

'I haven't got six million lire,' he said sulkily as he drank the brandy—which was in a wine glass filled to the brim. He wondered if he should explain to Lillian. But then he thought that perhaps she had done it on purpose. In which case, she was right. He could have drunk a pint.

'I haven't got six hundred thousand lire.'

'I know.'

'Give me the letter.'

Lillian handed it to him, and he stared at the offending and offensive sheet of paper, with its nasty little figures. He *didn't* understand it. He didn't want to.

'It's a plot,' he said. 'They're trying to drive me out of Italy. It's the communists.'

'Everyone pays this. On everything.'

'Not six million lire. Not just like that.'

'You should have been charging the film companies when you sent them the scripts back.'

'No one told me.'

'You're supposed to know.'

'Did you know?'

'Yes.'

'Well why didn't you tell me?'

'I thought you knew. And you always did the bills.'

That was true.

'I haven't got six million lire,' he repeated.

Lillian nodded sympathetically, and he tried another tack.

'How dare they!' he shouted, picking up the piles of scripts waiting to be translated and throwing them dramatically on the floor. 'They send me this rubbish, these cheap westerns, fourth-rate thrillers, pretentious political stories, things that no one would ever want to make or invest money in, and I translate them and add a bit of magic even to the dullest, the worst of them, so that some banker in New York or Berlin will read them and like them in spite of himself and—and—without me not one of them would be made, and thanks to me nearly all of them are. They get good actors who jump at parts I've translated they wouldn't do if paid a million dollars otherwise. They get good directors who see possibilities, poetry, they'd never have seen if it hadn't been for me. They couldn't have seen them, because they weren't there. I turn dross into gold, I—I *give* value, I don't add it. And they want to tax me! The film companies should pay. They should pay me. Six hundred million. For all the money I've made them. If they'd given them to some hack they'd never have made a penny. And they give them to me just because they know I'm a poet, I can touch things with magic, give value to them. They should pay me,' he said once more, wearily; and came to the end of his aria.

Lillian, who had heard this music before, though never quite so passionately sung, and in any case was busy picking up the hundreds of scattered sheets from the floor, murmured gently, 'They did pay you. All you had to do was forward the percentage that was for the value-added tax to the tax people.'

'Yes I know,' Wilbur sighed as he got down on his baggy knees beside her, to help her gather up the sheets. 'What am I going to do?'

'Well,' Lillian said, her own soft Irish voice suddenly infused with poetry, 'you could ask for a loan from Pam. Or someone,' she added, as a precaution.

Did she know about Pam's loans? And those of Jim and Betty and Bernard? Presumably. They all loved her—or said they did—and often invited her to tea or drinks. But whether it was because they did love her, or whether simply that they were checking up on their protégé, he wasn't sure. Possibly a bit of both.

'But not six million.'

'One and a half from each,' Lillian said quickly, revealing that indeed she did know, not wanting, in this hour of crisis, to be coy about it. But her grasp of mathematics was remarkable sometimes....

Yes. Probably if he explained how great an emergency this was, the four would respond. On the other hand, if they did; it would mean that he couldn't borrow anything else for a while, from any of them. And how would he live in the meantime? It might take a year or more before he could decently establish his pattern of Pam in August, Jim in November, Betty in February and Bernard in May. His mind fluttered helplessly round trying to find some different branch to land on. But Pam and Jim and Betty and Bernard were the only branches he knew of solid gold; the only ones who could bear his weight. So—there was nothing else for it. He would have to throw himself on their mercy, and worry about how to get through the rest of the year later.

'Where are they all?'

'Pam's here—'

'I know. I'm having tea with her this afternoon.'

'Betty's in Switzerland seeing her lawyers—'

'And having her face lifted,' Wilbur interrupted with unnecessary nastiness. But suddenly he felt terribly resentful of all the money she was throwing away on what was, frankly, a completely useless operation. One couldn't restore a ruin in a few hours....

'Jim's in Morocco— '

Spending a fortune on wretched little Arab boys, Wilbur nearly said, but didn't—

'And Bernard's in California.'

Distributing his wealth amongst his hundreds of children, grandchildren, nephews and nieces, all of whom were indecently rich already, and none of whom he liked.

'But they all should be back round the beginning of September.'

'When do we have to pay this wretched thing by?'

'Oh, not for a while yet,' Lillian lilted soothingly. 'It can wait until September.'

By the time the various scripts were back on his desk, and more or less in order—not that it would make a blind bit of difference if the odd fight in a western saloon got mixed up with some Italian policeman shooting down criminals, or two students making love while they discussed marxism got involved with a fat Sicilian lady swearing at her impotent husband—Wilbur was feeling calmer. He was still, as they finished sorting out the pages, muttering that it was a communist plot to drive him out of Italy, and that the government, yes the government and not the film companies, should pay *him* for the inestimable value he conferred on their more trashy national products, but the fire had gone out of the words now, and they were only a gentle refrain being sung behind the main vocal line—which was 'upwards and onwards dear child. Upwards and onwards. These are the crosses we have to bear.'

'Things could be worse.'

'Yes indeed they could. My God, Philip could be sick, or a hail storm might have ruined the flowers, or—something dreadful. No. These things are just sent to try us, but they are not really serious. Anyway—upwards and onwards dear child, upwards and onwards.'

And upwards and onwards they went, with Lillian straightening out bits of silver paper from chocolates, that could be used later to make collages, and Wilbur doing some weeding on the terrace. For the idea of work, after such alarms and upsets, was obviously out of the question.

TWO

Pam lived in a small 1890s villa on the outskirts of town. She lived there, in spite of her great age, great wealth, and various infirmities, alone, having only a cleaning woman come in the mornings, a nurse come to bathe her four times a week, and a gardener to tend her small and overgrown garden.

'How are you my dear?' Wilbur asked her, as he had on the phone earlier, when he arrived that afternoon; and Pam, as she stood waveringly under the art-nouveau lintel of her front door, said, as she had on the phone earlier, 'Oh, not very well.'

The reasons she gave this afternoon were different, however.

'My cleaning woman's on holiday, my nurse is on holiday, and my gardener's on holiday. I've been quite abandoned.'

'Oh Pamela,' Wilbur murmured, and stretched up to give her a quick kiss on the cheek.

He had to stretch up because Pam was immensely tall—almost seven foot—and he only gave her a quick kiss because there was something slightly blasphemous, or at least disrespectful, about actually touching someone as imposing, and awe-ful, as this towering old Englishwoman.

'You should have told me. I would have found someone to come.'

'Oh it doesn't matter,' Pam wailed piteously. 'It's only till Tuesday. It doesn't matter if I don't eat or wash for four days.'

She was perfectly capable of preparing her own food, of which there was always a vast quantity in the house, and

Wilbur suspected she was also perfectly capable of washing herself. She certainly looked and smelled clean enough, with her thin pale hair curling lightly round her white powdered face, her long tube of a body enclosed in a freshly pressed yellow flowered dress, and her air of eau-de-cologne and talc.

'Come in,' she said, and gave the front door a shove with the end of her walking stick as Wilbur moved forward. 'If you would be so kind as to carry the tea things into the garden, I thought we could have tea outside. It's quite shady out there, and cool.'

Wilbur doubted that; it was a terribly hot afternoon, he could see sweat on his nose, and his flapping unironed shirt and baggy once-white trousers were wet and clinging to him. He felt, in fact, quite wretched; and after last night's lack of sleep, the dramas of the morning, and a fairly winy if solitary lunch, he would have given anything to be siesta-ing at this moment. Especially since the tea Pam made was some exotic brand that always upset his stomach, and made him break out on the coldest winter's day. Still, he told himself as he went towards the kitchen, one did have a duty to one's friends, and if, after all, Pam was alone out here, it couldn't be too pleasant for her.

'Everything's ready on the tray,' Pam fluted down the corridor. 'I shall make my way slowly outside.'

Everything was ready; a silver tea pot, a silver water jug, two tea cups, sugar, milk, lemon, cream, a plate of English biscuits, two bowls of strawberries, and two lace napkins; but before Wilbur could pick up the tray, he had to scoop a number of ants from the cream, and remove one or two of the more obviously wormy strawberries. Pam had a great respect for life, and a great aversion to insecticides. Which was all very well, but for the fact that as a result her kitchen, and most of the house, was in a state of perpetual motion—particularly in the summer. And ants and worms weren't the half of it. The biscuits, if one looked closely, would be full of weevils, the floor alive with cockroaches, and every angle dark with mouse droppings. Not to mention the occasional scorpion and rat, and the clouds of gorged flies which were so fat they could hardly fly. The cleaning woman just about kept anarchy under control, though she was very short-sighted, extremely well-paid, and anyway under strict instructions never to kill anything; but whenever she was away, even for a few days, nature went wild. Wilbur remembered one other weekend in August, a few years ago, when he had come out to have tea with Pam. There had been a viper in her bedroom. 'Oh I *adore* grass-snakes,' Pam had hooted, as Wilbur had pointed the creature out to her, and she had surveyed it from her great height. Which was probably true, but neither here nor there, as Wilbur had felt obliged to remark. 'Well I don't know what I'm supposed to do even if it is a viper,' Pam had said huffily. And then: 'But do stop fussing Wilbur. You're turning into an old maid.'

Presumably, Wilbur thought as he lifted the now more or less lifeless silver tray and made his way through the kitchen door out into the garden, the snake had eventually gone away of its own accord. Though with Pam one never knew; she might, just, be keeping it somewhere; going to it at night and whispering to it in her high British voice; having it eat from her fingers....

'Over here,' Pam commanded; and Wilbur went towards a corner of the garden where a wicker table and two wicker chairs were set under a weeping willow, by the side of a mossy green fountain into which a cherub peed continually, and in which lily pads, frogs and goldfish fought each other for the limited space available.

'Will you pour please,' Pam said, as she stood and watched Wilbur set the tray down. 'And I shall lower myself into a chair. Did I tell you about my accident the other day?'

'Yes, my dear,' Wilbur murmured; but Pam pretended not to hear him.

'I came out here by myself to have some tea, and I was taking great care to sit down slowly. But the chair must have been on a *pebble* or something, because as I lowered myself into it it slipped backwards, and I went *crashing* to the ground. And there I was, absolutely immobile, because you know that once I'm over, I simply cannot move. I'm like a tortoise on its back, with all my little legs waving in the air. Or like that beastly insect in that story you lent me. It was really most amusing. Luckily there was a young man in the garden at the back here, and I called out to him and he came round and tried to pull me up. But you know when I'm like that I'm a dead weight, and though everyone thinks I'm just being tiresome, I simply cannot do a thing to help myself. Well the result was that this young man tugged on my arms once, twice, and then three times—and then fell over right on top of me.' Pam chuckled damply at the memory, and Wilbur wondered what psychiatrists would say about her little accident. Doubtlessly she had checked to see that there was a young man in the garden behind before sitting down so carefully in her unbalanced chair.

'Anyway, finally he did manage to pull me up, but I can tell you, it was quite a battle.'

Wilbur smiled encouragingly, and wondered how many more times he would hear this story. Several, probably. He looked up after he had poured Pam's tea to make sure she had made it safely into a sitting position today. But possibly because she didn't trust a fat sweating Wilbur to be as effective as a young Italian, she had managed quite successfully.

'Here, my dear,' he said, as he put her cup on the table between them—and as Pam added a coda to her tale. 'I'm all right as long as I'm absolutely vertical, and I'm all right getting out of bed, because I can push myself into a sitting position and then get to my feet. But once I'm horizontal, that's the end.'

'How did you manage last night?'

'I waited till seven-thirty and then phoned the greengrocer. He's done it before, and he knows how to come round the back and let himself in. But I shall have to be *most* careful over this weekend, because even he's gone away for three days. He said I was very lucky to catch him—he was just going out of the house. And everyone else round here is away. It's *so* pleasant and peaceful.'

'Well I shall be here all weekend, so if you do fall out of bed again, don't hesitate to call.'

'Oh I shan't. But I *shall* be careful. Actually—'

However before she could start again on the difficulties of remaining vertical, Wilbur thought it was time to change the subject—and to start leading the conversation round to a point where he could, very naturally, bring up the subject of the letter he had received that morning. He did hope Pam would get the picture immediately, without his having actually to ask. She probably would—she seemed in quite good spirits today, and unless she was in a particularly grim mood, she never did make him grovel too much. Just enough of course—but then she was very ancient, and very British, and, as they said, of the old school.

'Have you heard about the drought in England?' he interrupted. 'Apparently it's going to be a disastrous year for the farmers.'

That should do it, he thought. Because if the roof under which he sheltered was supported by the four columns of capitalism, and if, of these four columns, Jim represented commerce, Betty industry, and Bernard banking, it was Pam who represented the land-owners. She and her family possessed vast estates in England and France, sheep-farms in Australia, ranches in Texas, wheat-fields in the Mid-

West and forests in Canada; so that the mention of weather conditions almost anywhere in the world was always of great interest and concern to her, and a subject particularly dear to her heart.

Strangely enough though, today that didn't seem to do it. Because Pam merely sighed, said shortly, 'Oh it's always a disastrous year for farmers, whatever the weather,' and went back to sipping her pale and poisonous tea.

Wilbur sipped his, too, and wondered what else he could try.

'Have you been painting?' he offered—along with a bowl of strawberries, over which he poured some cream.

Pam accepted the strawberries, but refused the topic of conversation.

'No,' she muttered distantly. 'I don't think I shall be able to paint for a while. I have arthritis in my right hand, and I find it most difficult to hold my brushes.'

This was a new complaint, and Wilbur said, 'Oh my dear'; but he could see that Pam wasn't even interested in her arthritic hands—nor, for the moment, her painting.

'Actually,' she said again—and again Wilbur interrupted her.

'I got the most extraordinary brochure from the Royal Horticultural Society this morning,' he said. 'I meant to bring it to show you. There were some iris that you would love. I—'

But Pam, who was glancing disconsolately round her iris-less garden, would be interrupted no longer, or side-tracked onto any other subject but the one she clearly wanted to speak about. She silenced Wilbur by suddenly putting her hardly touched bowl of strawberries back on the wicker table, saying, with un-Pam-like lack of understanding, 'Ugh, these things are full of maggots,' and starting, with a great deal of pushing and levering, to raise herself to her feet. Wilbur made a move to help her, but she shook her head dismissively and finished the operation alone. Then, tall and tube-like, poking the ground with her stick, she wandered gingerly up and down the little gravel patch in front of him, and said, for the third time, 'Actually.'

Wilbur took off his glasses and started polishing them on his damp shirt. There was obviously nothing for it but to listen.

'I made a decision when I was lying on the floor last night. It's something I've been thinking about for a long time, but last night I actually made up my mind. And having made up my mind I intend to act without delay. I mentioned to you on the phone this morning that I should love to go to Australia again. Well, I should, though whether I will or not remains to be seen. But what I have decided to do is leave Rome.'

She paused, to allow the dramatic announcement time to sink in—which was just as well, because for a moment Wilbur was quite stunned. He put his glasses back on his nose and stared at the frail swaying woman, cool and pale in her overgrown garden. He felt the sky tremble over his head. Pam leave Rome. Pam leave Rome! She couldn't. She was far too old. She had been here far too long. They had known each other for too long. She was a part of Rome, just as he was. She was a part of his life. An essential part of his life....

Before he could say anything however, except, 'Oh Pam,' his tall old friend and benefactress continued. 'There's no one definite reason. Just a series of small things that add up to an overwhelming whole. First of all, though I hate to admit it, I'm too old to live on my own any longer. It's ridiculous and hateful to be terrified every time one's cleaning woman goes away for three days, just in case I fall over and can't get up. Or what would have happened if that young man hadn't been in his garden the other week? My voice isn't very strong, and I doubt if anyone would have heard me call out. I could have lain here all night. And I know I could easily afford to have someone come in and live with me and look after me. But (a) this house isn't big enough to have people living in, and (b) I've always loved it here just because I could live alone. I detest living with people, but if I'm going to have to, I don't want it to be here where I'd be continually remembering and regretting the days when I was alone. I should become hateful and unbearable. Then let's face it, the climate here is perfectly beastly. It's much too damp, which is dreadful for my asthma, and I'm sure that's what's brought the arthritis on. And if I can't or couldn't paint any more, I might just as well be dead. And then again—though I am old, and I'm going to move because I'm too old to stay here, I refuse to give in. If I did give in, well, I probably would stay here, or take a bigger house or apartment somewhere more in the centre of town, where I could have people living in who would look after me, and I could just lie back and be miserable. But no—' she raised her head defiantly towards the blazing afternoon sun '—I will not give in. I'm going to start a whole new life somewhere *completely* different. My first stop will be the South of France, where my younger sister lives. But I shan't stay with her for long. No. I intend to set up my own household, and though, as I say, I will have to have people look after me, that's a compromise worth making for all the advantages it will bring. And maybe I *shall* go to Australia. I'm sure Bobbie would love me to. But even if she doesn't—no Wilbur, it's time for a new life.'

Wilbur gazed at her in awe as she positively soared over him now, the whole wild band of the Valkyries riding and rejoicing in her old, drying veins. And even the look—the contemptuous I've-freed-myself-so-why-don't-you, won't-you, can't-you look that she cast down on him—was Wagnerian. He had never felt so tired, so grey, so over-weight, flabby, liquor-filled, out of condition, drab, in his life. It was as if Pam had suddenly, vampire-like, sucked his blood, his strength, and all his magic powers. And as if she too were aware of this, Pam went on, as she hobbled slowly back to her chair and began, even more carefully than before, to lower herself into it: 'But you know Wilbur, I must say if it hadn't been for you I doubt if I'd ever have found the strength or courage to make this decision. But you've always been so encouraging, always given me such hope, always made me realize that life must be lived, not just suffered passively. Must be taken in our hands and *transformed*. Well that's what I'm going to do. Transform my life. My whole world. And it's all due to you.'

'Well, my dear,' Wilbur finally managed to say as Pam's outburst subsided at last—as she herself did, into her chair—'I think it's wonderful. I mean I shall miss you terribly, of course. But—well—upwards and onwards. Upwards and onwards.'

'Oh dear,' Pam gasped, looking all at once tired out, and sounding more fluty and frail than ever. 'I'm so glad you approve. I was quite worried in case you vetoed the whole idea, and told me I was a mad old woman.' She started fumbling in the yellow handbag that hung from her arm, and after a while came out with a little white handkerchief with which she dabbed the sides of her mouth. She gave a little-girl laugh, and added, 'Well, I probably am a mad old woman, but that doesn't matter very much either, does it?'

'Not a bit. And you're not mad at all my dear. In fact I think—' and off Wilbur went, having gotten over his shock; giving Pam ideas, making suggestions, advising, amusing, and generally gilding her already glimmering dream. Doing, in other words, what he had always done and what he was so good at doing. Yet as he rattled on, giving the flying old lady shoves even further out into space, he was also leading up once again to a point where he could ask Pam—since this almost certainly would be the last time he'd be able to—to make him a final and most generous loan. A most, most generous one in fact—as, he decided while he talked, he might as well risk asking her for the entire six million he owed the wretched tax department. After all, what were six million lire to her? And if it really was due to him that she had found the courage to make this wild, magnificent gesture—then surely she owed him that, if not more. Much, much more.

For half an hour he built her up, until he had her fairly spinning. No poet had ever searched more desperately for the right word, no painter tried to find the exact shade, than he worked in that garden, with the sun beating down through the trailing willow fronds, and the wasps attacking the strawberries, Pam's freckled white arms, and his own sweating forehead. Fantasy after fantasy was tossed into the air, image after image; and he kept them all up there, juggling them with the most incredible dexterity, and never dropping one.

Till finally he—and he hoped Pam—was ready, and he ended his show with a shake of the head, an irritated flap at a wasp, and a long breathed-out sort of sigh.

'Well my dear, I can't tell you how much I approve and how I envy you. I'd love to do exactly the same thing. I really feel I've had it here. Twenty-five years is long enough in any one place. I feel I'm going stale here and—oh, everything just piles up.' He paused. 'Do you know this morning I got a letter from the tax department. It appears I was supposed to pay some sort of special tax on my translations. Have you ever heard such nonsense?'

'Oh, ridiculous,' Pam snorted. 'Just don't give them a lira.'

If this wasn't a promising reply, before Wilbur could go on to explain why he would have to pay—after all, while no one would ever put Pam in prison, or confiscate her household goods, or send her out of the country, they just might do it to him—and exactly how much he would have to pay, and that he was absolutely at a loss as to how he was *ever* going to find a sum like that at a moment's notice, the old lady had started talking herself again. And if the announcement of her departure had stunned Wilbur, what she said now made that shock seem like nothing more than the very mildest surprise.

'That reminds me,' she cooed, starting to fumble in her yellow bag once more, but this time coming out with a small notebook rather than a handkerchief, 'and this is really most awfully embarrassing dear Wilbur, but before I go—I do think we ought to settle our business, don't you.' It wasn't, remotely, a question. She opened the notebook and flicked through it, her 85-year-old eyes as sharp and bright as any efficient young secretary's. 'Now according to my calculations, I've loaned you some fifteen million lire over the years. I rang up my bank the other day and asked them to calculate the interest on that, but they said it would be *extremely* difficult what with inflation and devaluations and the changing value of money and all that. So I thought we could forget about the interest. That would be my going away present to you, I thought. But the principal—well, as I say, it's fifteen million, and I would be most grateful my dear if we *could* settle at a fairly close date. I do hate to have outstanding business, and I really *do* want Rome to be a closed book. I want everything to be neat and finished and over. And I know you've been doing awfully well lately. Lillian was telling me the other day that you're fairly weighed down with translations, and that you sold those two nice little Berman sketches *most* profitably.' There was an apologetic pause. 'And I hear that your dinner parties have never been so splendid.' A sigh, now. 'I did use to enjoy them *so* much, and I'm sorry I haven't been able to get out more in the last few years. But—I mean I realize that to pay the whole sum in one go might be a little difficult dear, but I thought if we could do it in three lots of five million lire each time, that wouldn't be too shattering, would it?'

Trickle trickle trickle peed the cherub into the fountain, and buzz buzz buzz went the wasps.

'It's not really for me that I'm so eager to get everything settled,' Pam finally filled the silence with, 'but I *am* quite old, and I can't live for ever, and I am very conscious of the fact that really I am holding everything in trust for Bobbie. It's for her, really, you see. And I know you think I am *fab*ulously rich, but it's not true, and after taxes and everything poor Bobbie—I mean, I must safeguard her interests, and I would so hate for there to be any bitterness between us if she discovered that—well, I'd been giving away what is rightfully hers.'

It droned on in the heat, that upper-class English voice that had been bred in mansions of polished wood and silver, that had been mellowed by centuries of tradition, that had been trained to command in the gentlest of ways, and been made sensitive by dreams of art. But Wilbur could no longer listen, no longer take in the words he was hearing. He was too dumbfounded, too flabbergasted, too hurt and beaten and betrayed even to try to. And this was someone he had thought of as a friend. Someone he had given some of the best moments of his life to, the ripest fruits of his creation. This was someone he had trusted, someone he had believed was basically good, who, despite all the advantages of her birth and upbringing, had managed in one way or another to get on the right side of the angels, and stay there. This was someone he had encouraged, exhorted, arranged shows of her water-colours for; introduced to all the people she would never otherwise have met but whom she professed to admire, worship and adore. And she dared to say that he was doing well, because he sweated out his life-blood every day on vulgar, ignominious translations—for which he was going to be taxed!—and had been obliged to sell those two little drawings he loved so much for a pittance. He was doing well because he gave splendid dinner parties. He had always given splendid dinner parties, always, even when flat broke, and never so splendid as the ones Pam herself had come to! She had heard—of course she had heard, as she sat alone listening to the whining wailing voices of bitterness and envy within her, listening to all those voices that always, only, told her of her own exclusion from a world not all the money on earth could have bought her, and condemned her to a world she had never had the courage to leave, however much she had pretended or even believed she wanted to. A world of falsity and exploitation and dull, crippling mediocrity. Oh, the Honourable Pam. This Regan! This Goneril! And he, the fool, had believed she was Cordelia. Oh the bitch. The cow. The false, faithless hag. He would like to kill her. Stick her head in that fountain and let her drown in cherub's pee, let her eyes be eaten out by frogs! Let her—

But since Pam had stopped talking, he did the only thing he could possibly do.

Which was laugh.

Not long, or very loudly. Just a quick, carefree laugh to show that it took more than a knife stabbed in his back and twisted round in his entrails to get him down. Fifteen million lire—plus six to the tax department. What was that? What was twenty-one million between friends? Six had been a problem. Twenty-one was a joke.

'Do you know, my dear, I really believe I'm psychic. Because just this morning, just before you phoned and I got that letter I was telling you about, I said to myself, "Wilbur George, it's time you got your financial situation straightened out." And I went through all my books seeing who owes me money and who I owe money to, and—well, apart from the fact that everything balances out almost to the nearest cent, when you phoned and said you wanted to talk to me I thought this is it. I'm going to settle everything with Pam. And then I was just going to bring the subject up—in fact I'd just started to—when *you* started. It's extraordinary, isn't it?'

'Yes, it's quite extraordinary,' Pam fluted, looking both relieved and—what? A trifle disappointed? Or merely apprehensive? Had she wanted a fight? Had she wanted tears and pleas; wanted at last to get her own back on her almost tame sprite who had always been just out of reach in the sunlight where she had longed to play—and felt cheated because even now he had slipped through her fingers? Or had she only been obeying the deepest dullest instincts of her shallow, dull soul—and was afraid that these instincts were being mocked? Who could tell—and anyway, who cared? If it was war she wanted, it would be war she would get. And she should at least know better than to go to war with a wizard. Start a new life indeed. Oh, the vanity of it! He would show her. She would never leave Rome. Never. And she would live long enough to regret that she had spoken to him like this, but no longer. He would concentrate all the most negative powers of his being on this seven foot tube of brittle bones and asthma. And all the dreams and fantasies he had tossed into the air before—he would let them fall to the ground before her eyes. Splat, splat, splat they would go, as they smashed with a squelch at her feet. And she whom he'd sent soaring into space—down she would come. Down face first to earth, to stare at the rank dark mud that was all her portion of that earth. Oh you lunatic Pam, he wanted to shout at her. You should never have done it. You should never have crossed swords with an enchanter.

While Wilbur was letting himself run on like this, and wondering, at the same time, exactly what legal steps Pam would take when it became apparent to her in a few days or weeks that he couldn't possibly pay her anything, Pam herself was starting to push up out of her chair again. Wilbur had never seen her so restless, and wondered whether she had felt the power of his reaction—perhaps he really could send out negative waves—or whether she was still feeling—as she had claimed to feel—embarrassed.

'Where are you going my dear?'

'Just to turn the hose on,' Pam hooted. 'With the gardener away, if I don't give them a bit of water they'll die before the weekend's over, my poor little flowers.'

'Shall I help you?'

'No, thank you. That's quite all right. I can manage I hope. Just as long as I don't bend over too far. And the tap's *almost* within my reach.'

Oh go on, bend over too far, Wilbur whispered silently to himself as he watched the old lady with a smile. Bend over and fall down on your back like a tortoise, with all your little legs waving in the air. Then I'll get up and wish you good afternoon and leave you here, and with everyone away and no one to hear you shouting, they won't find you till Tuesday. By which time you'll be good and dead. Go on, he shouted silently as Pam reached down slowly for the tap. Go on—another inch or two, and over you go. Go on! You could even, the silent voice, addressing Wilbur as if he were someone else altogether now, said, get up and give her the gentlest push. It wouldn't take much. Just a tap on the back, the tiniest bit of pressure—and she's away. Why don't you do it? She deserves it. And God, she'd have time to contemplate her errors. A whole weekend of lying on her back and staring up at the sky and surveying her emptiness and wickedness.... Why don't you do it Wilbur? the voice almost shrieked at him. Now. While you have your chance. Now. Now!

'Brava!' Wilbur cried, and 'There we do it!' the old lady

said, as water began to gush from the end of the hose, and she started to straighten up.

'You see, I'm not quite for the scrap-heap yet.'

She sounded triumphant, and her face was flushed with effort and pride.

'Oh Pamela,' Wilbur said—and lay back in his chair, feeling worn out. For a second, he realized, he had been carried away. He really wished death on the old woman. Of course, he told himself, he couldn't *really* have gone away and left her if she had fallen over, let alone actually pushed her. But still—even to wish death seriously on someone was dreadful, whatever they were or whatever they did. Because to wish for death was to deny life, and—

He felt a wave of depression sweeping over him, and stood up.

'I must go now I'm afraid my dear. We'll be in touch very soon about—business. All right? Just as soon as the banks are open again next week.'

'Oh there's no hurry,' Pam purred. 'Next week. The week after. I thought just as long as I can get everything arranged by the middle of September, I shall leave on the first of October. Do you think that sounds like a good idea?'

'That sounds like a splendid idea. Shall I take the tea things in?'

'Oh would you be so kind Wilbur. Thank you so much.'

Wilbur was so kind; only now the animal life of the kitchen which had seemed so Pam-like, so eccentric, so almost charming before, struck him as being just squalid, and wretched—and made him feel even more depressed. What *was* he going to do, he thought, as he watched the first ants rushing forward to check what had been left for them on the tray. What could he do?

'Wilbur?'

Pam's voice quavered in from the garden, and he went to the kitchen door and looked out. She was sitting down

again in her chair, wiping the sides of her mouth.

'Aren't you coming in?'

'No. It's so rarely I can enjoy real peace out here. And since I will be going away so soon I do want to take every opportunity—'

Wilbur walked out of the house and went over to her.

'You'll be all right out here?'

'Oh Wilbur, I come out here every day of my life.'

'All right then my dear. Look after yourself, thank you for tea, and we'll be in touch as soon as the weekend's over.'

'Yes. And thank you *so* much for being so encouraging, Wilbur. You don't know how much I needed it.'

'We all need encouragement,' Wilbur said as he bent over and kissed her forehead. He hoped he said it without any conscious irony or self-pity. Especially since, just at the moment, he wasn't feeling in the least bit ironical, or self-pitying. Only very, very depressed....

Nevertheless, and strangely, as he went round the side of the house, and turned to give Pam a final wave, a twinge of pity did come to him. Not for himself, however, but for Pam. Because she—who didn't see him wave—was sitting in her chair, staring out into her garden. And whether because she was thinking about leaving it, or whether because she was comparing its suburban disordered bohemia to the huge landscaped parks of her youth, and was wondering if this was all her dream and rebellion amounted to, she looked so forlorn and lonely and old that it was impossible not to feel a touch of sorrow.

It was only a touch though, and by the time Wilbur was in the road, walking towards the nearest taxi-rank—which wasn't at all near—he had forgotten all about Pam, and any regrets she might have. Because really, he told himself, his problems were both more pressing and of a more practical nature. What was he, what was he, what *was* he going to do? And, he wondered, on the assumption that there was never a second without a third—what final blow was fate going to deal him before the day was out?

THREE

If, by eight that evening, as he was setting the dinner table, he was no nearer an answer to the first of these two questions than he had been earlier, he did get an answer to the second. Though for a while it seemed more like a stroke of fortune than a blow of fate.

It took the form, this stroke/blow, of a phone call from Jim.

'James, where *are* you?' Wilbur drawled as he heard his friend's nervous, apologetic 'Hello?'

'In Rome.'

'Oh James, you're supposed to be in Tunisia till the thirtieth.'

'Yes, I know. Ha-ha.' This sounded like a laugh, but wasn't. It was just a sort of nervous stutter that Jim often gave whenever he was feeling excited, nervous, or guilty—which was most of the time.

'Well what are you doing this evening?'

'Nothing.'

'Do you want to come to dinner? I'm just setting the table.'

'I'm not alone, ha-ha.'

'Well it's not a street-urchin or a monster, is it?'

'It's not a street-urchin, no. But it might be a monster.'

'Where's it from?'

'America. New York City.'

'Oh it's sure to be a monster then. But bring it anyway. I've only got Louis coming tonight, and Penny Farthing.'

'Oh ha-ha-ha.' This *was*, presumably, meant to be a laugh. 'Penny Farthing. I do think that's funny.'

Jim had always found the name funny, and had always said so, ever since he had first heard it, years ago. 'Is she still as dreadful?'

'Now, James.'

'I've always wanted to write a letter to the papers saying that Rachel Sanders is Penny Farthing.'

'Rachel Sanders' was one of the foremost scholars of Etruscan art and civilization. Her real name was Penny Farthing.

'Now stop it James. It's much better to have someone enthusiastic like Penny, even if she does go on a bit, than some of the dreary young things you meet nowadays, who are always so surly, and never like anything, and can't even produce a simple declarative sentence.'

'I don't know what the monster from New York City will make of her.'

'Penny could hold her own against the combined forces of Manhattan, Brooklyn, Staten Island, the Bronx, *and* Queens.'

'Oh ha-ha-ha. Oh ha-ha-ha-ha-ha.'

'Now *James*.' Then, changing key: 'Can you be over around quarter to nine? Or is that too early?'

'No, that's fine.'

'See you in a little while then.'

'Yes. Bye.'

As Wilbur put the phone down, the cat, plump white and red, rubbed himself against his leg; and Wilbur leaned over and picked him up.

'Philip,' he said, kissing him, 'Uncle James is coming to dinner. And if we're very good and can get him properly drunk, we might even be able to ask him to lend us—' he divided six into three now—'two million. And then when Aunt Betty and Uncle Bernard come back—' He didn't finish his sentence. All the same, Philip seemed to understand, and purred appreciatively at this evidence of human ingenuity.

And surely Jim *would* lend him two million, Wilbur thought. Under the circumstances. And Betty and Bernard. Even if they loaned him nothing for the next two years. But at least that would take care of the tax department. Because, he decided, he wanted to get that debt out of the way first. Then he could concentrate on the more insurmountable problem of Pam; gather all his strength for what, he was sure, would turn out to be a far bloodier battle than any little skirmish with the State could ever be. Oh why hadn't she—and once again, he had a vision of Pam lying tortoise-like in her garden, while he stood laughingly over her, jeering, leaving her to—he checked himself, and quickly, putting Philip back on the floor, went to rearrange the table.

He had asked Jim and whoever it was he had with him to come at quarter to nine—a quarter of an hour earlier than the others—so that, assuming they were punctual, he would have a chance to sow the seeds that, either later that evening or tomorrow, would produce the hoped for crop. And punctual they were. But already, by ten to nine, he was regretting this move—and beginning to realize that far from there being any chance of harvest here, all he was likely to achieve was a blight and a freezing frost.

Because the person Jim had brought with him was indeed a monster; a tall, hairy, sullen young man with bad teeth and worse breath, who not only appeared to be impervious to the particular brand of originality of Wilbur George, but actually bored and irritated by it. He scowled, he shooed the cat away and said that the only use *he* had for cats was swinging them by their tails and smashing their heads against a stone, he looked at the picture-covered walls and said Wilbur must have some special affinity with and attraction to the third not to say fourth and fifth rate, and he looked at the beaded and winged clocks, the wild Rococo pelmets of the curtains that Wilbur had made with such effort from scraps of felt and velvet, and the sequined and gilded cabinets full of knick-knacks, monkeys, brown dolls and butterflies—and said Jesus, if there was a thing he couldn't bear, it was tack.

And all that Jim did—little jovial Jim, who was always becoming infatuated with young men of this sort; portly jolly Jim, who looked like a cross between Mr Pickwick and everyone's favourite uncle (though it wouldn't have been safe to leave one's nephews with him)—was, infuriatingly, giggle. Giggle, and gasp, and say 'Oh Chuck. Oh ha-ha-ha. Oh dear. You're going to hurt Wilbur's feelings.'

Indeed he was, and indeed he did; and by ten past nine, when Penny Farthing and Louis arrived to compound his misery, Wilbur was in despair. For not only had the third blow he had been expecting and fearing fallen—in the form of an announcement from Jim that he and the monster had come to Rome for one night only, and were off tomorrow on a trip round the world; which precluded any possibility of loans for months maybe—but also it became clear that the combination of the rude and shocking young thug—who for all his loathsomeness was no fool—and the lady Etruscanologist—who for all her seriousness was—was going to produce his second disastrous dinner party in two days.

It did.

Next day Wilbur stayed in bed. He cancelled his lunch and dinner parties, and didn't try to conjure the morning into life. He didn't want to. He preferred it dead. He lay in bed staring up at the wire and cardboard fishes that hung on threads from the ceiling, and refused even to think about the work he should have been doing. How could *anyone* behave in that way, he asked himself. How could anyone treat him like that? Of course the young man had probably had a deprived childhood and was very sensitive and only said nine tenths of what he did say in order to shock and try to prick the balloon of a world he himself aspired to but feared he would never attain, but—even so. To menace the cat, to break off a rose—no, it was unpardonable. Perhaps he should have ordered him out of the house. But apart from the fact that, having been told of the trip round the world, he had felt so numbed he wouldn't have had the strength to order a fly out of the house, he had been afraid that if he had done so, Jim—whose allegiance always lay with his temporary lovers, and never with his friends—would have left with him. Which while it might just have amused the little red man immensely, and prompted a telephone call this morning, before he set off, to apologize and to ask, by way of making amends, if Wilbur was 'you know, all right for cash', might also, for one could never really tell with Jim, have sent him off into a spin that would have kept him going round the world for years. As it was, with any luck the trip would end in disaster in some expensive hotel in Bangkok or Paraguay after a month or so, if not earlier. And while this might be too late to solve the problem of the tax-department—well, one did have to plan for the future, even at times like this, when the present was so black it seemed there might not be a future.

And then again, Wilbur asked himself: why had Penny been so particularly, so thunderously boring last night, droning on and on about her childhood, repeating herself, contradicting herself, and going out of her way to antagonize the unspeakable Chuck? Why had she insisted, when the young man told her he didn't do anything, on asking him what he *did*. It was obvious he was going to say 'push drugs, blackmail old men, rob old women and fuck anything that moves.' And why, when it was obvious, from what Jim had breathlessly and gigglingly interjected, that he and the monster had met recently in some unsavoury place in North Africa, had Penny so absurdly boomed 'Have you two been *friends* for a long time?' Of course the hairy young man had said 'No, just for two weeks. We met in a bar in Marrakech.'

And why why oh why, Wilbur asked himself, as he closed his eyes, unable even to bear the sight of his fish, had Ivy-League Louis, who was from New England and prided himself on being able to 'pull the team together', tried so pompously to pour oil on the troubled water by saying in his bossiest voice, 'Hey, come on you two. Let's not have any of this. This is a party.' Of course Jim had exploded with giggles, shaking and quivering over his cheese, and of course Penny had ignored him and said 'I remember the most *friiiight*ful party that Daddy gave one Christmas when he was in the High Commission in Hong Kong,'—and of course Chuck had interrupted Penny and stared at Louis and said, 'This is a *party*? Well Jesus, thanks for telling me. I'd never have known, and Jim, what the hell are you laughing at?'

Oh God, how he hated them all. Trampling through the magic and mysterious garden of his life, not once stooping to look at the flowers he had tended with such care, to wonder at the shrubs they had certainly never seen before. How *could* they? Just tramp tramp tramp, their eyes fixed on each other in hatred, and not a thought for the damage they were doing, for all the chances they were throwing away to learn something new, to feel something new, to explore the hitherto unexplored areas of their own souls. Oh, how he hated them....

And why, he ended this litany of despair, had Jim met that person and decided to go off round the world with him right now? Right now, when he was needed? Or the least he might have done, even though he hadn't been

ordered out of the house, was call up this morning before he left, and say—

But they had left at seven o'clock on a flight for Athens. . . .

However, the adage of there never being a second without a third having been seemingly confirmed, although Wilbur did spend the whole of that Saturday in bed, only getting up to feed Philip and water the flowers, by the afternoon a part of him was thinking, and finding relief in the fact, that at least the worst had happened—and no more blows could be expected. The situation was dreadful; but from now on upwards and onwards really was the order of the day, and not just a piece of empty rhetoric. He had had the operation, he told himself, and it still hurt like hell; but nevertheless, now he was convalescing.

This image of an operation and convalescence stayed with him all that night; and by Sunday morning had so given him strength that he was not only able, without the slightest effort, to bring the hot, quiet, bell-ringing day to life, but was even able to start making a first tentative assault on the mountains of translations that he had to scale. Of course he didn't allow himself to do too much, unless he suddenly found himself plunging back into despair, and of course he didn't allow himself to think of the tax-department's rapaciousness, Pam's betrayal, and Jim's desertion, but at least it was a start; and by *that* evening, aided by a particularly pleasant if small dinner party, he was feeling almost glad that these obstacles had been placed in his path; it would be a proof of his power, of his vitality, of his magic, when he overcame them. And overcome them he would, he vowed. Not only overcome them, but actually emerge more powerful, more vital, more magnificent from the struggle. Yes, he whispered to Philip as he kissed him goodnight—he almost *was* glad that he was being so tried. After all, what were three blows on such a towering tree of life? Mere taps on the trunk....

But after major operations complications sometimes set in; and so, sometimes, are adages and proverbs proved wrong. Because on Monday morning, still two further blows fell; and these, Wilbur realized, as he cancelled his social engagements for the whole week, and retired once again to bed—taking several bottles of whisky with him for company—were liable to floor him for good. Furthermore, they were blows of such a nature that he couldn't possibly believe that, if not the gods, at least the four members of his inner court weren't, for all that they hated each other, working in concert to destroy him. And he wasn't generally given to paranoia. But it was impossible for it all to be mere chance. There had to be some plan, some comparing of notes, some agreement that now, this weekend in August, was the time to strike. There also had to be, he decided, some liaison with the tax-department, some link there. Because that too wasn't possible.

Of the two further blows that fell, one took the form of a special delivery letter from Bernard, who wrote from California saying, in effect, that after all these lonely misanthropic years abroad he had suddenly discovered the joys of grandchildren and family, and had decided to stay on there, maybe just returning to Rome for a week in November to dispose of his apartment and arrange for the shipping of furniture etc.; and the other took the form of a telephone call from Betty, who said that he mustn't laugh, and it was hilarious, and when she had heard she had just *had* to call him and tell him because everyone else was acting as if it were a tragedy and only he would be able to see the funny side of it, but—you'll never believe it, and wait for it—I'm broke. Broke! Yes, me! Isn't it just too comic for words. Absolutely stony broke. Not a sou to my name.

Don't you think that's glorious, Wilbur. Old Betty, broke! Of course it's a mistake, she added quickly, and with a note of steel in her soft Southern drawl—any real suggestion of poverty being a little too risqué even for her boundless good nature and sense of humour—and it wasn't permanent, of course. Just terribly temporary. It was some silly lawyer's mistake in the complicated trust fund she had been setting up for her children, that had resulted in—well, it wasn't worth going into, and anyway she didn't have any *idea* how it had happened herself, and of course the bank was going to tide her over until it was all settled, but—

'You are all right Wilbur dear, aren't you?'

'Yes of course,' Wilbur murmured as he sat staring at the phone, unable to believe the words that were coming out of it, and feeling anything but all right.

'I don't mean healthwise. I mean—you know,' Betty laughed graciously. The merest idea of money always amused her ... 'Because I really shall be a little strapped for a while, and the banks charge such a terrible amount of interest on loans that I don't want them to give me more than's strictly necessary. Really I think my lawyers should pay, because it's their fault. But that'll mean suing them, and—well, we'll see,' she concluded coldly.

What could Wilbur say?

'Oh don't worry about me, Betty,' he cried, hoping to convey a hint of insincerity. 'I'm fine my dear, thank you.'

But if insincerity there was, Betty preferred not to hear it.

'Oh *good*,' she laughed, her soft grey voice rippling like a confederate flag in the wind.

'But what a bore for you.'

'I know. But it'll be an experience, and if there's one thing I've learned from you dear, it's to welcome new experiences with open arms.'

'How'd the operation go?' Wilbur asked solicitously,

knowing that Betty hated anyone to mention her efforts at restoration.

'I had to put it off for a few days, with all this going on,' was the slightly chilly reply. Then, since Betty's good humour really was unquenchable: 'And it's just as well. Can you imagine if I'd had to fight with my lawyers with my face all bandaged up. I might have done the old wreck permanent damage.'

'Oh, *Betty*,' Wilbur protested.

'Broke and broken,' Betty insisted.

'Oh Betty, you're impossible,' Wilbur sighed.

'Oh Wilbur, I adore you,' Betty cried.

Was it possible? No it was not. Again and again Wilbur asked and answered this question, as he lay grey and fat and sweating on his bed, sipping scotch straight from the bottle. Not even in a Victorian novel would such a sequence of events have been allowed. Even the most cynical author would have allowed a week or two to pass before hurling such similar thunderbolts at his poor suffering hero. And then there wouldn't have been four—or five, if you included the letter from the tax-department. Two, or three at the very most. But to have everything come crashing down over just one weekend—no, it was too much. It *wasn't* possible. That *did* presume the existence of an organized plot. And again and again, and with ever more insistence, Wilbur returned to this theory; until, by the time he had finished the first bottle of whisky, he wouldn't have abandoned it for anything on earth. There *had* to be some concerted plan to get him, and there was. But what had he done, he asked himself plaintively, to deserve such a fate? All right, he did, to a certain extent, sponge off Pam and Jim and Betty and Bernard; and all right, he did it—generally—in the name of an art he hardly practised any more. And yes, perhaps he did give too much importance to his social life, and should have forced himself to take time off and really sit down and finish a novel, or a collection of poems, or something.

Yet—he wasn't an evil man. And Pam and Jim and Betty and Bernard *did* have more money than they knew what to do with. And though it was easy to say, and perhaps a little hard for the philistines to take, his very way of life *was* an art, even if he didn't set it down on paper or canvas. And though his social life was immensely, possibly too important for him, it *wasn't* an empty, vacuous social life, involving dressing up, gossiping, going to night-clubs and being 'smart'; all shallow show and pathetic pretence. He really did only have his dinner parties because he cared about people, and felt that people—the unlikeliest people, the most assorted people—somehow blossomed and were touched with a sort of magic under his roof; discovered lights in themselves they didn't know they had, heard music they had never heard before; saw views they had never dreamed existed. He *did* have the gift of stirring life in the lifeless, giving hope to the hopeless—and even exorcising devils from the possessed, and unhappy. He made the unimaginative dream, the complacent question themselves, and the joyless laugh. And surely *this* was the work of the poet—even if a world that gave too much importance to the product and not enough to the production, that cared too much for the eternal and not enough for the merely mortal, didn't consider it as such. So why—

But there was no answer. And though all that had happened might be impossible, it had, nevertheless, happened. In one long weekend the entire structure of his life had collapsed. And as he lay in the ruins, with his sheets clinging to him and the whisky bottle in his hand, he told himself that while there were only two ways out for him now—one, by more or less giving up his social life and finding, if he could, some mundane, serious, and hopefully well-paying 'job', and the other by continuing as he was but doing translations every day of his life from morning till evening until exhaustion or liquor got him (for he knew that if he really worked like that, only a continuous flow of liquor would sustain him)—both ways were so alien to his nature, so depressing to contemplate, that he refused to do so; and would continue to refuse at least until Lillian came tomorrow morning. In the meantime—he would, as he had on Saturday, stay in bed. Only today, unlike Saturday, since there was no earthly chance of anything cheering him, he would get as drunk as he possibly could.

He got so very drunk in fact that when Lillian—and Aida—did come the following morning, he told them he was sick, and sent them home; though whether because he did feel too sick to cope with them, or whether because he was still nowhere near ready to make a decision about his future, he neither knew nor could be bothered to think about.

And still he stayed in bed, and didn't even answer his phone when it kept on ringing, all afternoon and evening. Why should he, he thought, as it rang for about the twentieth time. It could only be more bad news....

If he had answered it however, as he discovered next morning when Lillian, remarkably, burst in on him at eight o'clock waving a newspaper in her hand, he wouldn't have heard altogether bad news. Not bad for him, anyway. What's more, though his faith in popular saying had been shaken by the five rather than three blows that had fallen on him, he wouldn't have been able to resist—as he wasn't that morning—saying to himself as a first reaction that even the darkest clouds had a silver lining.

Because Lillian, as she ran into his bedroom saying, 'Oh Wilbur, I tried to call you all yesterday afternoon and last night, but you were never in,' and 'Have you heard the news?' and 'Oh, it's terrible,' eventually calmed down enough to inform him that Pam, poor Pam, poor, dear, kind, sweet, gentle old Pam—was dead.

'Oh my God no,' Wilbur cried, trying to look as distraught as Lillian sounded—and leaping out of bed as nimbly as a ten-year-old. 'Oh, how dreadful.'

'Oh, it's awful.'

'I'm so shocked I don't know what to do. Get me a glass of brandy, dear child.'

'I tried to get in touch with you, but you weren't in.'

'No, I was out. Oh, my God. Poor Pam.'

'Oh, it's awful.'

'A brandy, dear child.'

'Her maid found her yesterday morning.'

'She was so *happy* when I saw her Friday afternoon. And she seemed so well. She was talking about starting a whole new life. Oh dear. Poor Pam.'

'Oh poor Pam.'

'Poor *thing*,' Wilbur agreed.

It was another five minutes before Lillian could be prevailed on to bring him a brandy, and another fifteen before he was able to sit down with the newspaper and read the details of 'the old Roman resident found dead.' But when he had done so, he started, at last, to feel genuinely upset himself. Partly because he had known and been very fond of Pam for so long, and was sorry that she was dead in spite of the way she had behaved the other day, and partly because of the manner of her death. For it seemed she had fallen over in her garden while bending to turn off the hose, had broken her pelvis, been unable to get up or move, and had lain on the flooded earth for at least twenty-four hours before the end had come; on Saturday night, it was calculated....

'Oh, how dreadful,' Wilbur whispered again, though quite sincerely now, and felt himself going pale. He remembered how intensely he had wished just that death on Pam. And he was a magician....

But worse was in store. And as he read on to the end of the article, upset was hardly sufficient to describe the emotion he felt. Because there was a peculiar and poetic detail about Pam's death that the paper reported at some length; a detail that was terrifying....

Apparently Pam, as she had lain on her back in her garden, had tried to leave a last message on the gravel path on which she had fallen; a message which she had scratched with a small stick, but most of which had been washed away by the still gushing hose. All that remained in fact, according to the paper (and it was strange that she had written her message in Italian) were two words: 'Viva il—'. What could that last word have been? 'Duce' was the one that sprang most immediately to mind. But unless the old lady had lost her mind as she lay there (which was possible), and had suddenly been carried away by a fit of nostalgia for the Mussolini it was said she had once admired, it wasn't likely. No, the journalist who wrote the article said. Surely it was more probable that this grand old character, who had lived such a long, varied, and interesting life, had written some positive message on the gravel when she had realized that her time had come. 'Viva il mondo', maybe. Or 'Viva il sole'. It was heartwarming to think so, anyway....

What was terrifying to Wilbur about this was not so much the report itself of this mysterious message, as the photograph of it some enterprising newsman had taken. Because from the photograph one saw that Pam hadn't actually written 'Viva', but had abbreviated it in the Italian fashion. Had scratched, therefore, simply a large W. So her message read 'W il—'. Which might mean 'Viva il' to everyone else, but to Wilbur, at least, were quite clearly the first three letters of his name....

He shivered. Oh yes. He was a magician. He had willed that death on Pam—and she had known it. And in her last moments she had tried to accuse him of it. What was more, she had possibly even succeeded. So that if it hadn't been for the hose washing the gravel away, at this very moment the police—

'Another brandy dear child, please. Quickly.'

Lillian obviously saw the urgency this time, and brought the brandy immediately. 'Are you all right?' she whispered, sounding surprised by the intensity of this delayed reaction.

'Yes, quite all right,' Wilbur gasped. 'It was just that I was asleep when you burst in and I couldn't really take in what you were saying. But—oh dear.'

'Do you think her daughter's been told?' Lillian asked, becoming calm now that Wilbur had taken the burden of dismay on himself.

'I don't know, dear child. Perhaps you'd better call the British Embassy and find out.'

'Shall I do it now?'

'Yes, I think that would be a very good idea,' Wilbur murmured, eager to be alone for a while. 'And if they haven't, find Bobbie's name in my book and send her a cable.'

'Right,' Lillian said, and went away; and, 'Oh, how dreadful,' Wilbur whispered, yet again, to himself.

He had killed Pam, of whom he was very fond. He was an artist and a magician, and with his art and his magic he had killed her....

Oh, how dreadful....

He really *was* a magician though, a tiny and hesitantly self-satisfied voice—the voice that he had heard in Pam's garden the other day—breathed inside him. He really did have power, it went on slightly louder—not having been told to shut up. And he who had thought—admittedly on Saturday, before the two further blows had fallen, but nevertheless—that these disasters had been sent to try him and that he would overcome them, was being proved right. He *was* going to overcome them, the voice inside him practically cheered now. Of course he was. And having overcome them he would be—oh what would he be? Only that which he had always been. But more obviously now, more dazzlingly. Magnificent. A master. A genius....

The blood rushed back to his head and he thought he was going to have a heart attack. He had never felt so intoxicated in his life. Never so wildly, exaltedly drunk. And it wasn't the brandy that had done it, either. It was his own blood. It was his own spirit. Yes! It was that that was intoxicating him, making him fly, swim, sparkle, shine. And while he was truly sorry that Pam was dead, and while he had been fond of her—dear, crazy, dotty old Pam—he was also thrilled beyond words at this proof of his power. He, who could give life, could also take life. He who could bless could also curse. He who could create could also destroy. He was more than a magician. He was a god! He was—

And then, just as he had last Friday morning, when sitting on his terrace, he got a hold of himself. Oh, you silly old fool, he shouted. You stupid, weak-minded, wicked old man. And shut up, he roared at the hysterical voice burbling and cackling inside him. Good God! He was going mad. Just because he happened to have imagined Pam's death—and it wasn't difficult; it was a very risky thing for her to do, stay in the garden by herself, and was certain to end in tragedy sooner or later—he started believing he had caused it. Wicked, vicious, stupid old man! And if Pam had started writing his name in the gravel, it was probably because, being a mean old bitch as well as a dear dotty old thing, she had been trying to leave a message to Bobbie about the money he owed her. It was also quite natural, since, being almost the last thing she had spoken about before she had had her fatal fall, it was the only thing that had stayed in her frightened and befuddled brain; been the only straw of reality and safety to which she had hoped to cling as she was swept outwards on the hose water into the dark dreamlike sea of her own death.

Of *course* that was the explanation, and really he must get a grip on himself and not allow himself to have such insane fantasies. Magician indeed. God. *Really*.

But you did want her to die and will her to die, the voice inside him said sulkily.

Yes I know, Wilbur muttered, not wanting to shout at it again, and searching for—and finding—a compromise. But that doesn't mean to say I killed her. She just happened to die in the way I'd planned. No. Not planned. Fantasized about. All right?

All right, the voice said, sounding a little sly, and smug; as if realizing that, not having been banished completely, it would always be able to speak again, make a comeback, at some future date.

The British Embassy had informed Bobbie of her mother's death, and the following morning—Thursday—she arrived in Rome.

That afternoon Pam was buried in the Protestant Cemetery.

Wilbur took Lillian to the funeral, and sent her home in a taxi afterwards. But he stayed on. And when the rather small band of mourners—most of Pam's friends were either dead, out of town, too old to go out in the August afternoon, or didn't want to be reminded of the fate that awaited them all, soon—had disappeared, he took Bobbie's arm, and they walked arm in arm round the peaceful, pleasant graveyard.

'Mother always wanted to be buried here,' the tall, fair, and very sensible woman said, looking at the green almost English grass, the flowers, and the tall dark trees.

'One couldn't have a nicer place,' Wilbur murmured, uncertain as to what tone to adopt in the circumstances.

'Thank you so much for all your help.'

'Oh, my dear,' Wilbur breathed.

'I didn't put you out asking you to stay on, did I?'

'Of course not.'

'It's just that I do want everything to be settled as quickly as possible, and you *were* mother's closest friend, and so I thought—oh, you know. You might be able to tell me if she wanted any little thing to go to some special person. And what to do with her paintings. And, oh, you know. Everything. But I really don't want to take up any of your time. I know you're always terribly busy.'

'Oh, my dear,' Wilbur—who hadn't done a stroke of work since last Sunday—repeated, patting Bobbie's hand.

'Also there's one thing in particular I wanted to talk to you about. You see mother made a very simple will about forty years ago, leaving me everything. Which is all very well, but also—well, a little mean, I can't help thinking. After all, I'm not hard up myself, and I lead quite a simple life, and I'm not likely to have any children myself. And she really did have a fair amount of money. So what I thought—and this is what I'd like your advice about—is that I'd like to set up a foundation or something for young writers or painters or composers. Something that was close to mother's heart.'

'I think that's a splendid idea,' Wilbur said, wondering for a second how young the young writers and painters had to be.

'You don't think it's foolish and sentimental, and that it might not be better just to give some large lump sum to various charities?'

'Oh, I think a foundation would be a far better idea, though admittedly I'm prejudiced. Really, my dear, the world is quite bad enough as it is. But without art it would be delivered totally into the hands of the barbarians. And then not all the charities in the world could feed the hungry or look after the sick. First things first. And after all,' he concluded, becoming quite passionate now; but he *felt* quite passionate, 'not to be too pompous about it, art is life and discovery and exploration and revolution and movement and all that, and carries all the rest of the world in its wake. Without it there'd only be armies and money-making and death.'

Bobbie laughed, and read the inscription on Keats's tomb, to which Wilbur had led her as if to underline his point.

'All right, you've convinced me,' she said. 'I mean I almost was convinced anyway, but I thought that maybe—'

'Oh no, my dear.'

'There is one other thing,' Bobbie said, looking down at the ground now, and then bending over to stroke a white cat who was lying in the flowers. 'I mentioned about giving some little things to some of mother's friends. But also—well. I saw the photograph of the gravel where poor mother was lying. And I know the papers said she was trying to write Viva il something. But that sounds like a lot of nonsense to me.'

Wilbur, who had been about to bend over and stroke the white cat himself, stiffened and looked instead at the silvery stone pyramid at the back of the cemetery, where St Paul had been martyred.

'I'm sure she was trying to write your name.'

'Oh,' Wilbur said.

'And if she was, the only reason I can think of is that—well, as I say, you were her closest friend. And I know she was terribly grateful for everything you did for her over all these years. So I'm sure she was trying to tell me something.' Bobbie stood up again, and smiled. 'Not that I needed telling. What I mean is, I'd like you to accept a gift, Wilbur. But you mustn't think it's from me. It's from mother. I know that's what she wanted.'

'Oh my dear, I couldn't,' Wilbur demurred, trying not to flush—and trying, also, to silence the little voice within him that only yesterday he had tried to banish, which was starting to howl with laughter. Oh the irony of it, it cackled. You wizard you. You number one enchanter of the western world.

Shut up, Wilbur told it.

But it had been right to be smug, right to realize it would make a comeback—even if it hadn't realized this comeback would be so very soon—and it wouldn't be so easily silenced. Oh, you magician you, it howled. You magician....

'Oh come on. Don't be coy with me please,' Bobbie said.

'Well then, thank you my dear.'

'Is there anything of mother's you particularly like?'

Wilbur smiled. 'Well there is that little silver monkey....'

'Oh Wilbur, you're too much,' Bobbie laughed. 'Of course you can have it.'

And have it he did. And two Georgian silver candlesticks. And an inlaid enamel eighteenth-century French musical box. And inside the musical box, carefully folded, a dollar cheque for the equivalent of twenty-one million lire....

And that, Wilbur thought a week later, having seen Bobbie to the airport—she had been a virtual whirlwind of activity, and apart from the sale of the actual villa, which was in the hands of an agent, had done everything there was to be done, and disposed of all that was disposable—was that. His problems, at least for quite a while, were over, the tax department could be paid, and he could quite easily sit with his feet up until Jim returned from his trip round the world, Betty sorted her finances out, and Bernard—as Wilbur was certain now that he would—got sick of his family, and changed his mind about settling in California. Not that he did sit with his feet up of course, and in his own whirlwind of activity actually managed to get through all the translations he had been neglecting for so long, and start on several new projects as well. But just the idea that he was free for a while gave him strength and energy; just the knowledge that his problems were over made him work. He did decide, however, that some time in the winter he would take himself off on a long holiday, to somewhere he had never been. To somewhere, possibly, where no one had ever been.

Oh, how happy he was, he told himself. And *what* an artist he was!

And that would have been that—but for the fact that on the fifth of September—a Monday—he received three letters. They were, naturally, from Jim and Betty and Bernard, and all of them said almost the same thing. Which was that they had not only gotten his note telling them about Pam's death, but they had also gotten other notes, from other friends in Rome, telling them about Pam's death. And included in those other notes had either been a photograph, cut from the paper, of Pam's last message, or an exact report of it. And they, like Bobbie, were quite unfooled by any theories of Pam's madness and Viva il whatever. Only they, who knew Wilbur better, did not interpret the first three letters of his name as Bobbie had done. They *knew* what Pam had been trying to write in the gravel....

'Oh, you wicked old thing,' Betty wrote from Davos, 'you killed her. Oh Wilbur, I adore you. But you *are* naughty.'

'You murdering old motherfucker,' Bernard wrote from San Diego. 'Why the hell didn't you do it years ago?'

'I wish you were here,' Jim wrote from Rio. 'You'd be able to dispose of the *creature* for me.'

They all of them enclosed a cheque in their letters; Betty for five hundred dollars, Bernard for seven, and Jim for one whole thousand....

FOUR

Wilbur was on his terrace when he read these three letters, and though it was a glorious morning, with the September sky startlingly blue after the whiter days of August, the sun warm and kind, and the colours of the city softer and more harmonious than they had been just a week or two ago, he couldn't help feeling a stab of winter in his veins, and seeing a cloud of grey shroud over the domes and terraces and roofs. Because if all the events of the past few weeks, with all their ups and downs, had been, however exaggeratedly, just episodes in the comedy of life, these letters were something quite different, and belonged somehow to quite another world. An unsettling, disturbed, slightly nightmarish world. For while all three of them seemed to treat the subject of Pam's death—Pam's murder—in the lightest, airiest way, as a great big joke, there was, beneath their easy tone, a sort of menace. Possibly because murder, however one laughed about it after, couldn't really be made a joke of, and possibly because neither Betty nor Bernard nor Jim, under their various exteriors, were really light or airy people. They hadn't gotten where they were, nor stayed where they were, by being light and airy. And while of course all three of them might just be teasing, not seriously thinking for a moment that he actually had killed Pam, he was fairly sure that none of them were. Otherwise why would they all, without a comment, have sent him those cheques?

What was more; while it could—looking back on it dispassionately—have been mere chance that in the space of just a few days in the middle of August he had not only

found himself falling flat on his face, but also having himself stamped on simultaneously by all four of the people he relied on, it wasn't, simply could not be mere chance that he had now received these letters all on the same day, all saying the same thing, and all announcing mutely that he was going to be stamped on no longer. Of course there could be an explanation; he had written himself on the same day—to Bernard in California, Betty in Switzerland, and Jim c/o the American Express in Rio (Jim had said before he left that they would be passing through Rio, though he hadn't said when)—and they had all written back on different days—Jim first, Bernard second, and Betty last—but even so, that just wasn't good enough. And while before, when he'd been attacked, he had favoured the theory that his friends were acting, however improbably, in concert, now he no longer did. Now he suspected that the simultaneous arrival of the letters depended not on any planning—which in any case would have been extremely hazardous, owing to the erraticness of the mail—but on some sort of not divine intervention, because he didn't, when it came down to it, believe in any divinities, but the intervention of what he could only call the forces of magic, or the efforts of some particularly neat artist. That had to be it. And that was what was really scaring, and really made grey winter fogs seep out of the invisible fractures of the clear September sky. Because art and life seemed to have become confused. Of course he had always held that they couldn't be divided, but even so—

It was scaring in precisely the same way as it had been scaring to read of the manner of Pam's death. But while he had been able to get over that particular fright quite quickly, acquit himself of any blame there without too much effort, these letters, or the attitudes of their writers, wouldn't, he was afraid, be so easily shaken off, explained away. To make matters worse, since all three of his friends did, without any apparent doubt, believe that he *had* murdered Pam, now even that ghost rose again from the dead and came to haunt him. *Had* he killed her, he asked himself once more. Not literally, of course, but just by sending out such waves of hatred from the chemical box of his brain that she had, left alone with them in her garden, been powerless to resist them—her only revenge being the writing of the name of her killer in the gravel? Had he, the artist and magician, done that?

No he had not, Wilbur said sternly to himself, and stood up. He was a great believer in the powers of the human brain, and undoubtedly that unpleasant looking lump of matter was capable of remarkable feats. But to kill people—no. That was going too far. Though—and now he sat down again, and felt somewhat less stern—witch doctors were apparently able to kill people—even if just by inspiring them with so much fear and self-hatred that they died by themselves. Was that what he had done to Pam then? Made her realize just how shabbily she had behaved, so that shame and mortification had knocked her over? Or had she behaved shabbily, and talked of a new exciting life, simply because she knew her own, which hadn't been quite as brilliant or exciting as she would have liked, was over?

Oh, he didn't know. But he did wish she hadn't written that message, whatever it meant. And he did wish that Betty and Bernard and Jim hadn't written those letters to him.

The only thing he didn't wish in fact was that Pam would come back to life. Because, he couldn't help telling himself, much as he was grieved by her passing, her death, which couldn't have been delayed much longer anyway, really had solved a number of his more pressing problems—and looked, if the evidence of the three cheques were anything to go on, as if it were going to go on solving even his future problems. After all, frightening or not, winter-bearing or otherwise, five hundred plus seven hundred plus a thousand *did* equal two thousand two hundred. And two thousand two hundred dollars were not to be sneezed at, even if they had been gained, as it were, by false pretences.

That day, for the first time in twenty-five years, Wilbur wrote two poems. He didn't plan on doing them—they just came to him as he sat at his typewriter. And they came to him, he had to admit—bright, allusive, deceptively slight and subtly deep—really rather well....

He wrote several more poems in the days that followed; and while wondering about the mysterious springs from which art flowed, paid the three cheques into his account....

However, if the next three weeks—full of parties and poems and even a start on a painting—passed so pleasantly and quickly that he was almost able to forget that there was an unidentified and possibly blight-bearing worm in the rose of his life, the first of October brought him a reminder; a reminder that came, as he had been afraid it would, with the return to Rome of one of his three friends. And oh, he told himself, he had been right to feel disturbed, and apprehensive.

First because Jim—for Jim it was—had hardly stepped off the plane before he came puffing and chugging round to hear exactly what had happened to Pam; and second because —and this was the greater cause for alarm—when it came to it, Wilbur found that he was unwilling, for some reason, to admit that he *hadn't* killed the old woman. He didn't actually say he *had*—but he let the assumption drift in the air like cigar smoke in a closed room. He just didn't feel like opening the window....

Quite why, he asked himself afterwards, he really wasn't sure. Because it added a touch of drama to his life? Because he liked, at least in his dreams, to wear exotic clothes?

Because Jim expected it of him and he hated to disappoint people? Because it enhanced his reputation as a magician and an artist? Perhaps it was for all of these reasons. Or perhaps it was only because he had an illogical feeling that if he did come out and positively state that he hadn't killed Pam, even if Jim didn't ask for his thousand dollars back, he wouldn't be so forthcoming about advancing any more when the time came. And however bright the financial picture of one's life was at the moment, one could never tell what might happen, and when the time *would* come....

But if he didn't tell Jim precisely how his afternoon with Pam had ended, he did tell him everything else; how Pam had described the very way she was so shortly to go, how—and this involved admitting that Pam had been lending him money, which was still another cause for misgivings later—Pam had asked him to pay her back what he owed her, how he had been tempted to give her a push as she was standing up to turn the hose on, how she had talked about her new life, and how she had said she didn't want to go back inside when he said he had to leave; wanted to stay out and savour the peace and quiet....

He described it all brilliantly, creating that hot August afternoon all over again there in his living room; making the willow weep, the cherub pee, the gravel crunch beneath his feet.... He conjured the whole scene up until it was palpable, until Jim himself could see it there, in front of his eyes, as clearly as if he had been hiding behind a bush and peeping through the leaves. He was, in fact, as he rewove the fabric of that day with the flimsiest of materials—mere words—quite dazzling; and Jim was suitably dazzled. He sat enraptured, chortling and chuckling, his little knees pumping up and down in excitement.

'Oh ha ha ha,' he cried. 'Oh I do think that's funny Wilbur. Oh poor Pam. Oh ha ha ha ha ha.'

Wilbur sat there modestly, and made no comment.

'And they didn't find her till the Tuesday morning. Oh poor Pam. Oh ha ha ha. Oh you must do something about Chuck.'

'Well, tell me James,' Wilbur said, glad for a chance to change the subject, 'now I've told you all our little local news, how did the trip round the world go?'

That sobered Jim up immediately, and he seemed to find nothing to laugh at there. On the contrary, he became quite indignant at the very mention of the past few weeks.

'Oh, don't talk about it. Psychotic little whore. We went round the entire world in twenty days. Sixty countries. Three hours here, two hours there. I think he was hoping I'd collapse. And it wasn't as if he didn't want to do anything when we arrived everywhere. Oh gosh no. It was rush here, rush there, in and out of taxis, museums, churches, temples, shops, bars. Good God, it was dreadful! I think the longest time we spent anywhere was in Paris. Thirty-six hours.'

'Why didn't you ditch him somewhere?'

'I tried to, but he always seemed to have my passport in his pocket when I needed it.'

The memory brought a little colour to the Pickwickian face, and a shake to the shoulders; but one couldn't have called it a laugh....

'Well, where've you been for the last few weeks if your trip was over so soon?'

'Oh, resting in Mexico City. He decided he had to go back to New York to see his poor old mother. But he's coming here tomorrow. Oh dear.'

'Does he have money?'

'He should have. He robbed me blind.'

'But what does he want from you, James?'

'Oh *everything*, I think,' Jim almost sobbed. But then, suddenly, he recovered his normal high spirits. 'You ***must*** do something Wilbur.'

'I'll put a spell on him if you like.'

'Oh, that would be wonderful. Turn him into a tortoise. Oh yes. Oh—' and off he went again into paroxysms of laughter, as he thought of Pam lying in her garden.

'I think you're very mean James, laughing like that.'

'*I'm* mean? Oh heavens. Oh Wilbur. Oh—oh—oh—' And now Jim was reduced to tears of mirth, and for a full minute was bent double on the sofa where he perched. Finally, though, he gathered himself together enough to gasp, 'Oh I'd love to have seen her expression. And then writing your name like that on the gravel. She might have had you arrested, vindictive old bitch. Though I guess—'

'Bobbie had *quite* another interpretation of those letters,' Wilbur interrupted tartly. '*She* thought Pam wrote my name because I'd been her closest friend and wanted to remember me. In fact,' he added, 'Bobbie gave me those candlesticks there—and that silver monkey, and an eighteenth-century French musical box.'

He didn't mention what had been inside the box; he thought it wiser not to....

Jim stayed for another half an hour; laughing, talking, and still visibly excited by what he thought Wilbur had done; though it wasn't till he was leaving that he said, once again, 'You must do something about Chuck for me.'

'Oh, come on James,' Wilbur smiled, steering his friend towards the door. 'My spells are precious. I can't just toss them around. And you're quite capable of taking care of all the Chucks in the world yourself.'

'Oh goodness yes,' Jim puffed, and laughed; though what Wilbur had said was no more than the truth. In fact, of all the various young men with whom Jim had been involved since Wilbur had known him—and while some were even worse than the dreadful Chuck, some had been really quite pleasant—hardly one had survived to enjoy the money that they had managed to squeeze out of the dapper little man.

Some had taken to drink, some to drugs; some had been smashed up in the fast and expensive cars Jim had bought them, some gone mad and killed themselves. There was even a story that Wilbur had heard somewhere—he couldn't remember where—that once there had been some young man who, having money himself, and being genuinely and disinterestedly attached to Jim, had actually been murdered in rather obscure circumstances. Though whether this was true, Wilbur neither knew nor cared to know.

'And come to think of it,' Jim continued, 'there are several people I'd much prefer you to turn into toads before Chuck. Or for you—oh ha ha ha—to go to tea with.'

'That's quite enough of that James,' Wilbur said, almost pushing Jim out the door now.

'Betty for instance,' Jim chuckled, as he started walking backwards towards the elevator. 'Or Bernard. I can just imagine—'

'James!' Wilbur said.

It was only much later that night, as he lay in bed going nervously over the events of the day, and trying, unsuccessfully, to get rid of the strange little lump of unease that he felt growing within him—a little lump that was liable to swell into something monstrous, he felt, if he couldn't get rid of it—that Wilbur realized he had forgotten to ask Jim a question he had meant to ask him. Which was why he had sent that cheque....

However, if he didn't ask Jim, he did ask Betty, who, three days later, was the next of the three remaining pillars of his establishment to come to see him—and hear the details of Pam's death. Not that he received a satisfactory reply from her.

'It was very sweet of you my dear,' he said, as they sat together on his terrace, 'but really, you shouldn't have.'

'Oh Wilbur,' Betty purred graciously, if a little uncomfortably. 'I was so worried that you might not be all right, and I thought after I phoned to tell you about all that mess the lawyers made that it was awfully silly of me, because you would never have said if you needed anything. And I just couldn't bear the idea that you were in Rome by yourself and might be—in difficulties.'

'Well anyway, thank you,' Wilbur said, feeling uncomfortable himself now, and regretting that he had ever mentioned the matter. What did he expect Betty to say? That she had given him that money because she had guessed that Pam had pressed for the payment of her debts—and didn't want him to interpret her temporary freezing of funds as a prelude to a like action on her part? In case she, too, met with an unfortunate accident....

'But I must say my dear,' he went on, clearing his throat and looking up brightly, 'you're looking wonderful.'

'Yes, I think they've done quite a good job this time,' Betty laughed, touching her tight, taut skin with her hand, and then adjusting the white silk scarf that covered her piled up, youthfully golden hair. 'Though I do regret not having my teeth done while I was about it.'

Betty's teeth, which were very slightly irregular, had been a constant source of regret to her for as long as she had known Wilbur, and presumably longer; and every time she went to have alterations made to her person she swore that *this* time she was going to have her mouth *really* fixed. But every time she returned from Switzerland or Paris or wherever, nothing was changed; and Wilbur guessed that now—for Betty, though not quite in Pam's class, was no young girl herself—it never would be.

'Oh, you can't change them,' Wilbur, who was as perfectly trained in certain responses as a very devout nun, cried. 'My God, it's wonderful having a whole set of one's own teeth,' at your age was tacitly understood, though not said, 'and the second you start letting them mess about in your mouth, that's the end. Within a year they might all be perfect. But they'd all be false, too.'

'Oh you're so right, Wilbur,' Betty sighed. 'Give me the genuine any time. But come along now, don't let's talk about me. I want to know exactly what you did to that awful old Pam.'

'My dear, I didn't do a thing.'

'Oh come now. Look me in the eye Wilbur George, and tell me the truth. You can't fool your old Betty you know.'

'My dear, I swear,' Wilbur started, trying to beat down the temptation not to disillusion Betty, 'that I only—' he paused, and hesitated. 'Put a curse on her,' he ended quickly, feeling ashamed of himself for his weakness.

'What sort of curse? Just the tiniest nudge as you were saying goodbye to her?'

'Oh Betty—'

'Oh Wilbur, you know you can tell me. And I don't know what she did to you, and I'm not about to ask, but she was such an evil old creature, in spite of her lavender water and her being the Honourable Pam, that I'm sure it was something beastly. So you were absolutely right to do whatever you did. I would have done it myself if I'd ever seen her.'

Say 'I did nothing, absolutely nothing,' Wilbur shouted at himself. But to Betty, with a mischievous twinkle in his eye, he simply said, 'Oh my dear.'

'No. Don't try and get out of it,' Betty insisted with a knowing smile and a bejewelled and admonishing finger waved in the face. 'No "oh Betty's". Just the plain truth, you wicked thing.'

He made one last try. He told himself that he was mad, that this wasn't in the least bit funny, and not even to one's closest friends did one admit to murder; especially to murders one hadn't committed. He told himself to stand up and walk away, leaving Betty alone on the terrace with her slightly irregular teeth and youthfully golden hair. He told himself to be rude. To be witty. To tell Betty a joke. Even to tell Betty the truth.

But he couldn't. He was helpless. And as if his mouth had a life of its own, he felt it opening—and heard words coming out of it.

'Well, my dear, I mean even though I was fond of her in a way, Pam really could be very poisonous. And that afternoon she said something that was—well, just terribly hurtful. And I don't know what happened to me, but something just suddenly snapped, and I thought here we are sitting in this lovely garden, in this beautiful August afternoon, and even if the whole world couldn't be like this, it could certainly be much more like it—if it wasn't for the evilness of people like Pam. And really we don't live long enough, and have to accept quite enough compromises as it is, without putting up with petty, withering meanness. And I was looking at the birds and thought I quite genuinely would put a far greater value on the life on one of those sparrows than I would on the life of this old woman here. And when people are mean and sour, it *isn't* just themselves they're hurting. They're damaging the whole world, making it even more difficult to live in than it already is. They're defacing an already extremely badly damaged painting, devaluing an already nearly worthless coinage. And it's so easy just to stand aside and let it happen, and then shrug one's shoulders and say, well I couldn't have done anything anyway. One *can* do something, always, and one has a positive duty to stand up for life and everything that's on the side of life. Otherwise the dust and the greyness will creep up and overcome one, and then it's simply not worth bothering. And so, as I say, there I was in this deserted garden with this wretched old creature who was practically draping cobwebs over the flowers as I listened to her, and I thought I will not stand for this another second. I will not put up with it.

Otherwise I'm putting up with disease and suffering and cruelty and hatred. And so—and so Pam had already told me what would happen to her if she fell over. And there was no one about. And so—and so—' Wilbur repeated, and suddenly stopped, overcome by his speech; which had moved him and come out quite as genuinely as if it had been true.

And Betty, too, was moved. She was breathless with emotion, her white scarf fluttering softly in the autumn wind, her hands folded demurely in her lap. And after Wilbur had finished she allowed almost two minutes to pass before she spoke; before she almost gasped, her voice overhung with Spanish moss and awe, 'Oh, you're absolutely right my dear. You're *so* right. My God. My God!'

He wasn't right at all, Wilbur thought miserably; if only because it was a weird sort of logic that argued that one could claim respect for life while taking it.

But Betty was either not too keen on logic, or wasn't, when she wanted something to be true, remotely interested in it; and simply continued to sit in her chair—rocking slowly back and forth now—and whisper to the gold October afternoon and Philip-the-Cat, who was gazing at her, beady eyed, 'Oh, you're so, so right Wilbur. You are. He is right, isn't he Philip? He really is.'

And then, with a suddenness that shocked Wilbur—and Philip—she stretched over, grabbed the cat, held him to her bosom, and fairly shouted, 'My God, Wilbur, look. This cat's beautiful. And he wouldn't be beautiful if there were any meanness and littleness in him. And heaven knows he's old enough. No. It's only we humans who wither and become haggard—because we *accept* meanness, give in to it. We make ourselves ugly, and we make the world in our image. If we left it to the cats and the birds and the flowers, my God it would be better. It would be *beautiful*! It *would* be. Isn't that so, Philip,' she sobbed, 'isn't that so, Wilbur?'

Wilbur, who was alarmed by this unexpected evidence of

lunacy in Betty, wanted to tell her to put Philip down, in case she hurt him. But he was feeling too worn out even for that—and all he could do was murmur, like an echo of the woman herself, 'Yes, my dear. You're right. You're absolutely right. You're so, so right.'

A few minutes later when Betty, still gliding on winds of high emotion—she said she just had to go home, and *think*—left, she kissed Wilbur gravely on both cheeks; and added a postscript to the overcharged and exalted talk on the terrace. 'My God,' she said, 'and we're not talking in abstract terms either, are we? Because the world really *would* be a pleasanter place if just one or two other people we know were to follow Pam. All the terrible, *triste* people we know. Blown away like dust. Whoooof! Oh heavens, how beautiful it would be. How very, very beautiful....'

That the one or two other people Betty would have blown away were Jim and Bernard, Wilbur had no doubt at all.

FIVE

It stood to reason that, since Jim wanted Wilbur to remove Betty and Bernard from the face of the earth, and Betty, Bernard and Jim, Bernard would want him to dispose of Betty and Jim. And so, when he returned, on the fourteenth of October, to Italy, grumbling and grousing about California, his family, his health, modern youth, and the advent of world communism, he did. Only he, unlike the other two, didn't wait to suggest it as a parting shot when Wilbur went to see him. In fact, it was his opening shot.

'Well, you old shit,' he cried in his strange voice, that was both squeaky and gruff at the same time, as he slapped Wilbur on the shoulder, 'I was hoping by the time I got back you'd have killed that old queer Simpson and that Southern whatever the opposite is of belle Betty. But there's time, and you certainly fixed Miss lavender scented Pam. Good for you. I never thought you had it in you, you Tennessee turd. What are you drinking?'

'Scotch and water, you old fool, and I'm not from Tennessee.'

'Well, Missouri, Mississippi, Louisiana, wherever the hell it is.'

'Carolina.'

'Carolina my ass. Anyway, it's good to see you again, and how are you doing apart from your killing?'

It always took Bernard, who was very fat, had shoulder length white hair and a little wispy beard, who had once, somehow, been an officer in the Indian army and never quite gotten over it, and who barked and swore and played the part of a grouchy old misery in order, he claimed, to frighten the young, a little time to remember, when they met, that Wilbur himself was not part of that particular age group.

'I'm doing all right,' Wilbur said non-committally, tempted to tell Bernard at least about the irony of fate, and Bobbie's gift to him. He knew he would have appreciated it. But after a second's reflection, he decided against. It *was* better to keep certain things secret....

'You got my cheque?'

'Yes, thank you.'

'I thought I'd better send you something as soon as I heard what you'd done to Pam. 'Cos I presume you killed the old bitch because she wouldn't give you anything. Or did she ask for her money back?'

'Oh Bernard,' Wilbur murmured.

'Don't be coy with me you sonofabitch. I've known what you've been doing for years. And good for you, too. But I thought just in case you understood my letter as meaning that you couldn't soak me for any more, I better get some cash in the mail right away. Otherwise you'd have gone to work with your lizards' legs and your adders' tongues and your little wax effigies, and I'd have had a heart attack right there in California, with all my milk-fed offspring spewing over me. Jesus!'

'I thought you loved it out there, and were happy to see them.'

'Summer madness,' Bernard growled. 'Summer madness. But I don't know what the hell we're doing standing in the hallway here. Come into the living room and tell me all the gory details.'

And since it was useless to pretend with Bernard, or be coy, or try any more to make any contact with the truth, Wilbur, sitting in his friend's dark, old-fashioned living room, with its leather furniture and black beams, its books and rugs and gloomy seventeenth-century paintings, did just that. He told Bernard exactly how he had killed Pam, down to the smallest detail. He told of the surprised little cry she made as he pushed her. He imitated her long, hooted, 'Oh Wilbur, now don't panic. Just give me your hands and pull me up very slowly.' He described her fluttering, surprised more than frightened expression as she realized he had no intention of giving her his hands; and had indeed pushed her on purpose. She had been more like a butterfly, he said, as she lay there, than a tortoise; a butterfly with wounded, useless wings. And finally, with downcast eyes, he told of the noise he had heard as he had left that hot, overgrown garden. The noise of old fingers, scrabbling desperately in the gravel....

'You might at least have turned the hose off,' Bernard cackled, his little eyes glistening behind his spectacles, and his tiny very white hands tugging at his wispy beard. 'Jesus, it must have been uncomfortable.'

Yes, Wilbur thought. It must have been....

'What would you have done if someone had found her in time? She'd have had the police on you in a second.'

'Oh, of course she wouldn't. If there was one thing that Pam loved it was a bit of violence. She used to phone me every day to make sure I'd read about all the latest murders.' Once again he imitated Pam's voice. '"And according to the *Herald Tribune*, there were bits of brain all *over* the damask covers." No, actually I think after the first shock had worn off, she approved thoroughly of what I'd done. It was the biggest kick she'd ever had in her life, being killed.'

'And the last.'

'And even if she had been found and had gone to the police, no one would have believed her. Everyone knew she was a dotty old thing. They'd just have thought that the shock had really turned her brain.'

'Well anyway, I think it was about the smartest thing you ever did in your life,' Bernard muttered. 'Though God knows why you didn't do it years ago. Never could understand what you saw in the old hag. Apart from her money of course.'

'You're not a lover of human nature in all its diversity as I am. And Pam was an original, for all her faults.'

'Well thank Christ for that. I'd hate to think of any more like her around.'

'Oh Bernard,' Wilbur said; and tried to think of some more convincing reason to give him why he had liked Pam so much. And he *had* liked her—just as he liked Jim, who underneath his huffing and puffing and his boring infatuations with unsuitable young men was one of nature's innocents, and just as he liked Betty, who in spite of her relentless charm and the occasional lapse into lunacy was one of the kindest, most *enthusiastic* people he had ever known. And if there was a thing he appreciated, it was enthusiasm.

'She loved life,' he finally came out with. 'Even if she didn't really have enough—I don't know what—courage, maybe, to go all the way. Or maybe she'd been too messed up by her childhood to really be able to escape it. But she tried, and that was what was important.'

'Oh Jesus, you sound like some sloppy columnist,' Bernard barked. 'I hope becoming a murderer hasn't made you sentimental. *Every*one's been messed up by their childhood.'

'Well then, in the last analysis she was on the right side of the angels. *Ecco*. Does that satisfy you?'

It might not have satisfied Bernard; but it did make him laugh a harsh, caustic little laugh. 'That's where we'll all be if we're not careful of you,' he croaked.

'Oh, you old fool,' Wilbur said.

If he had liked Pam, and did like Jim and Betty, Wilbur also—immensely—liked Bernard, who, he considered, in spite of his manner and the act he put on, was one of the softest-hearted, most sentimental of beings. In fact, he was probably closer to him than any of his other friends, or to anyone else in the world. The trouble was, he liked him so much, and the couple of hours he spent with him this afternoon passed so easily, amused him so greatly, and so carried him away into his role as a killer of old and helpless ladies, that it wasn't till he left him, and emerged from that dark and gloomy apartment into the bright early evening of the city, full of cars and people and movement, that he started, once again, to have doubts about this role, and this charade he had set up. And even more serious doubts now than any he had had before. Because if, with Jim and Betty, he had simply strung them along as it were, let them believe what they liked about him without actually coming out and saying 'this is so', with Bernard, now, he was really into it. It was no longer a matter of lying by default. Now he was really lying. And of course it *was* only a game, a silly charade. But if he suddenly decided to quit the game now, say 'all right, that's it, it's been fun while it lasted but not a word of it is true,' would anyone believe him? Or was he going to be stuck with his role—and stuck with it not only for the present, when it was or seemed amusing—but in six months time maybe, or a year; when it might neither be nor seem amusing any more. When it might, all at once, become horribly serious. What would happen if he fell out with Betty or Jim or Bernard, he wondered? How would they use their knowledge against him? Or even if he didn't fall out with them, how would they act towards him? Because even if they weren't aware of it, they would be affected by this discovery of a hitherto unrevealed trait in his character. They couldn't help but be. And that being so—wasn't there a danger that, instead of being merely the court magician and the fool, he might become a sort of slave? Oh yes, there was, he thought, as he raised his hand for a taxi, and then lowered it again quickly and decided to

walk home. There was a very real danger indeed.
Oh why was he such a silly old fool, he asked himself. Oh why was he? And what *had* he got himself into....

SIX

He wasn't really sure if his friends' attitude towards him did change over the next three months; but he couldn't help but be aware that his own attitude to them did. Not only to them, but in small, insidious ways, to the whole of his life.

Because while, after those first meetings with Betty, Jim and Bernard no mention was ever made of Pam, and of what he had supposedly done to her—apart from the tiniest, most veiled allusions when he was alone with one or other of them—he found that he could no longer totally relax in their company; no longer be his own, magic self. And sometimes, when he sat with them and started to tell his stories, build his marvellous gothic castles in the air that were—or had been—so real that one could stretch out one's fingers and touch the stones, could walk down cold flagged corridors, could stand on the parapet and catch sight of the most breath-taking views, or open great heavy doors and suddenly find oneself in the most splendid, painted ballroom, blazing with candles and alive with characters in masks, he became terribly aware that now not only had he failed to conjure up even the flimsiest wall, but was doing nothing but repeat tales he'd already told—and repeat them, inexcusably, without the slightest variation. He started to feel like an old actor telling of former triumphs; whose mind and imagination, however, had become too weak even to get the dates and details right, let alone convincing; so that what had once caused laughs and ohs and ahs, now just caused embarrassed glances, and shifting on seats, and hands being mutely examined.

What was worse, if this was so on those occasions when one of the Three was present—and one of them generally was; he felt obliged to invite each of them to lunch and dinner at least twice a week now, whereas before it had sometimes been only once every three weeks—he found it even more so when none of them were. Which was appalling. To have new faces, old friends, sitting irritated and uncomfortable round his table, clearly thinking, 'who is this sad old man I've heard so much about, who everyone claims is so brilliant but is just rather tiresome', or 'oh dear, poor Wilbur is getting tired, and a little sad; next year when we come to Italy maybe, for the first time in decades, we'll give Rome a miss', was humiliating and depressing. Also, he told himself, as flat disastrous dinner party succeeded flat disastrous dinner party, there was absolutely no reason why—at least with everyone else—he should be like this. All right, with Betty and Jim and Bernard there was, however ridiculous it might be, some sort of explanation. But with the others, there was none. And yet it happened; happened in spite of all his efforts, and in spite of the fact that he had never lavished so much time and money on his entertaining. Yet even his cooking was dull and uninspired now, and he seemed suddenly to have acquired the knack of buying wines that were too acid, or too sweet, or just didn't go with the meals....

It happened so often in fact that by the end of November he was starting to entertain less; telling Lillian to say, when people called, that he was out of town, or wasn't well; or even, simply, that he was sorry....

He should go away, he told himself, as he had planned to do. But just because his magic had deserted him so thoroughly, he didn't have the energy to decide where to go, or to buy tickets, or to make arrangements; and besides, he kept on thinking that there was no point in going away while he was depressed, and that maybe tomorrow's dinner party would be better, would signal a return to his old form, and *then* he could go. But tomorrow was always worse than today; until he got to the stage where it was the day after tomorrow he put his faith in; and then three days from now....

Yet of course there was a reason why everything had become so grim, and why he was so unlike himself in everyone's company, and not only that of the Three. And though he pretended not to be aware of it, he was finally forced to be. Forced to admit that he was being choked by that lump of unease that had taken root in him that day when he had seen Jim on his return to Rome. An unease that never left him now, day or night, and took the form of an image of Pam lying helpless on her back in the gravel, writing his name with a stick. And while it was entirely his fault that it was growing in him, this lump, and while all he had to do to eradicate it was tell the truth—he still couldn't do it. Not even at the risk of losing all his friends, and of having the entire, elaborate construction of his social life crumble down around him.

Was he going mad? he asked himself. Possibly. How else could one explain such folly? How else but on the theory of madness—or on the even more unsettling theory that he was afraid that if he did tell Betty, Jim and Bernard the truth, they would once again, just as they had in August, desert him? More than once this second idea—this shameful, pitiful idea—came to him, before, having rejected it and rejected it, he finally took it in and held it up for inspection. And when he did he was horrified by himself. My God, was he really continuing this game just because he was frightened of losing his financial support? Sure, most people had to debase themselves to earn money—but in such a way? Oh, it was dreadful. And yet, having once taken the idea in, he couldn't get rid of it, however dreadful it might be—and was finally forced to confess to himself that this indeed was the truth. He couldn't tell his three friends that he hadn't killed Pam—

and was suffering these feelings of guilt and unease as a result—just because he was scared that if he did they would no longer, when the money they had lent him and the money Bobbie had given him were gone, give him any more. That was all there was to it.

He tried to be cynical, to laugh at himself. He tried to tell himself he was a wicked old man, but that nevertheless he was on to a good thing, and if all it involved was admitting to something he hadn't done—well, that wasn't a very stiff price to pay. He might have had to work in an office, or in a factory, or down a mine. But he couldn't manage it—mainly because this fear of losing his backing was so irrational itself. Why on earth *should* his three rich friends desert him if they learned he hadn't killed Pam? There was absolutely no reason for them to at all. God knows they had been doing it long enough, without his having to kill anyone for them. And yet—and yet—they had sent him those cheques when Pam had died, as if to assure him that their temporary absence from Rome was only temporary; assure him that *they* had no intention of behaving like Pam. In fact Bernard had said as much. So—

The other reason why he couldn't really laugh at his baseness was the one that had been with him from the beginning, and that was that he honestly didn't find murder funny, and he had the feeling that all this pretence, that had begun so lightly, couldn't but end in some bad, not to say terrible way.

However, in spite of his unease, and in spite of the flatness of his dinner parties, these weeks before Christmas did have their compensations. For he found that, whether because his magic powers sought another outlet now that that of his dinner parties was closed, or whether because, with Bobbie's money, he was, for the first time, ahead of the game as it were, and therefore wasn't obliged to do so much in the way of translating, more and more, when he went into his study and sat down at his work table, instead of concentrating on those translations he did have to do, he was doing some work of his own. It had started with the poems; it progressed with some short stories; and got to the stage that, one day around the beginning of December, without any conscious effort on his part, he found himself starting a novel that he'd been meaning to write for years. And strangely, the worse his dinners went, the better he wrote; to the extent that he even began to wonder whether his sudden inability to entertain his friends didn't at all depend on any feelings he had about Pam's death, but simply on the fact that his energy was being absorbed in another, more private way.

Not that he was entirely happy, if happy at all, about this change of course in his life. Because it was all very well conjuring up castles on a blank page, hoping to cast his spell eventually on some unknown reader, but he missed not being able to do it in his daily life. He would have liked, of course, to have been able to do both, but as it apparently wasn't possible, he wasn't at all sure that the one made up for the other. Did his sudden ability to write again really make the unease he felt worthwhile? He doubted it....

He was so very doubtful in fact, had such very mixed feelings, that a week before Christmas, as he sat writing in his study listening to the shouts and noise of a communist demonstration going past in the street under his house—and wondering if there were any significance in this, too; as if his own particular crisis were being echoed on a larger scale by these chanting workers and students—he decided, rather than risk a fiasco on Christmas Day—and his Christmas dinners were famous, were the very highlight of his whole social year—he *would* go away; go away to some quiet and grand hotel, and there, in peace and solitude, make up his mind about just what he was going to do with his life.

* * *

And so he went—though not to any unexplored land, as he had dreamed of doing. He went, instead, to Paris. He took a suite at the Ritz, and went out every day to the very best restaurants in town. He bought himself, for the first time in years, some clothes and shoes; and he bought, in little shops in funny parts of town, knick-knacks that he thought would look well in his apartment. (Though, also for the first time in years, he found, as he did so, that he wasn't altogether sure of his taste; and was afraid that what looked so very much like his sort of thing in Paris would turn out to be, when he took it home, simply ugly, vulgar—in Chuck's words—tack.) He went to Fauchon's and bought the most exotic foodstuffs; he went, every evening, to the ballet or opera, sitting in the very best seats. He stayed for two weeks, and spent a fortune; and realized, by the time he left, that he had come not only to enjoy himself—which he tried to convince himself he did, but didn't; his unease wouldn't leave him even here—and to make a decision as to what to do about the farcical but unpleasant situation he was in—and he did come to some sort of decision—but also, and above all, just *to* spend a fortune. To get through as much of his money as possible, in the shortest time possible; so that he would be *obliged* to test his theory about what Betty etc. would do if he did tell them the truth.

The decision he came to was this; that since he couldn't go on in this way, even though it did seem to inspire him to write, he would, as soon as he got back, confess that he had lied to just one of the Three—Jim, probably, since he had lied less to him than to the others, and therefore his reaction wouldn't be too humiliating—and then, immediately, ask for a loan. And if—as of course he would (he would, wouldn't he?)—Jim came through with the goods—well, he would know that he really had been mad to think as he had, and would immediately go to Betty and Bernard and confess to them too. If Jim, on the other hand, refused the loan—but no. He couldn't. It was impossible. It didn't bear thinking about. He *couldn't. . . .*

Yet he did.

He sat pink and sulky in the library of the small settecento palazzo where he lived, glancing every now and then towards a door behind which the dreadful Chuck—who was still very much around—presumably lurked, and puffed indignantly.

'Oh good heavens Wilbur, you can't need any more at the moment.'

'James dear, you know the cost of living is going up every day,' Wilbur said, trying to keep the misery and the now atrocious unease he felt—an unease as painful as a toothache—out of his voice.

'Well you should cut down on your expenses. You can't entertain as you do every day.'

'I have cut right down. I didn't have a single person for lunch or dinner for four days before I left.'

'Well *I* didn't notice. And anyway, you seem to have had a jolly good holiday in Paris.'

'James, I have to get away occasionally. And I spent almost nothing there. I stayed in the most modest little hotel in the Boulevard Raspail, I only ate in little local bistros, and I didn't buy myself anything.'

'That's not what I heard,' Jim muttered petulantly.

'Well I don't know who's been telling tales, but you shouldn't believe them.'

'I can't believe anything any more. First you make up some ridiculous story about killing Pam, then you tell me it's not true, and now you tell me my cousin Susan and her husband didn't see you on three separate occasions in Paris in places that were anything but local bistros.'

And he thought he had avoided them so cleverly after he had caught sight of them in Le Grand Vefour. God, Wilbur asked himself bitterly, why must the rich have spies and cousins everywhere, checking up and reporting on any intruders in their gilded world....

'I did *not* tell you I killed Pam, James. I've never heard such nonsense. You know perfectly well I am not in the habit of murdering people. I thought you were joking when you talked about it. I mean—you were joking. It was all a silly story.'

'I don't see why,' Jim pouted wretchedly, nodding in the direction of the door. 'I'm sure *he's* killed lots of people in his life. Maniac that he is.'

'But I happen not to be Chuck, James.'

'Well you're almost as expensive. And I really can't let you have anything at the moment. The stock market's awfully low, and what with one thing and another'—once again, a vague nod towards the door—'just for the present things are very tight. Besides, he'd kill *me* if he found out.'

'I do think you should be a little more careful in your choice of young men, James,' Wilbur said, unable to keep a note of real savagery out of his voice now. 'And I really don't think it is any of Chuck's business what you do with your money, and you certainly shouldn't make your friends suffer because you happen to have some delinquent in tow.'

It was, of course, quite the wrong thing to say, and only increased Jim's sulkiness.

'He's not a delinquent. In fact, potentially he's an extremely intelligent person. And he can be immensely charming when he wants to be. And I'm not making you suffer. You just can't live beyond your means. Why should you? No one else does. Besides—' and now Jim, either afraid that this discussion was turning into a nasty scrap, and wanting to avoid any further unpleasantness, or because he genuinely found the idea amusing, suddenly gave one of his little chugging laughs—'even if you don't think that it's any of

Chuck's business what I do with my money, he most certainly does.'

Shake shake shake the little shoulders went....

'Oh James,' Wilbur cried; and then, made desperate by the implications of this conversation, blurted out 'well would you lend me some if I told you I really *did* kill Pam?'

'Oh for heaven's sake Wilbur, make up your mind,' Jim murmured; and then, after a second's reflection, started to laugh again. 'But I suppose if I really did think you had, I'd have to, wouldn't I? Oh ha ha ha,' he burbled, completely cheered up and his old self again. 'Oh really Wilbur. But you didn't, did you, so that's all there is to it. I couldn't really believe you had before, but on the other hand, one never does know in life, does one?'

Then, popping up out of his chair like a little Jack-in-the Box, Jim bustled to the door and opened it, calling 'Chuck! Chuck! Wilbur didn't kill Pam. You were right.'

'I told you,' came the detestable young man's voice back. 'That old Southern phony couldn't kill a fly. He's just full of shit.'

'Oh ha ha ha,' Jim went, glancing nervously over his shoulder at Wilbur. 'Oh Chuck, really, don't be so rude. Oh dear. Oh I'm sorry Wilbur. Oh good heavens. Oh ha ha ha.'

But Wilbur was too sunk in misery, too much in the throes of panic to be stung by any insults, or, really, to hear them.

So it was true. If he did tell the truth, he wouldn't get any more money. And while he still had a little left, after his extravagance over the last month or so, particularly in Paris, very soon he wouldn't have. Well, in any case he supposed it didn't matter, because unless he recovered his powers as an enchanter, he wouldn't be entertaining much anyway. But on the other hand, unless this almost irresistible urge to write his own things that had afflicted him lately—and he thought of it now as an affliction—left him, he wouldn't even be able to do enough translations to pay for the basic necessities of life; Philip's food, the rent, the electricity and telephone, and Lillian—who was, though she couldn't type or take shorthand, nor do anything else a secretary is meant to do, a necessity nevertheless; if only for the calming influence she had on him.

'James my dear,' he said quietly, 'why have you loaned me money for all these years then, if I should live within my income? I never have, ever, and you've never complained about it before. And I was never expected to kill before to earn my keep.'

'Oh don't be so silly Wilbur,' Jim snapped, returning once more to petulance. 'I *was* only joking about Pam and all that. I mean I never really did think for a moment that—' a brief pause, for a brief shake of the shoulders '—no, that's not true. I really did think you had. But honestly Wilbur, that's nothing to do with it.' He closed the door again suddenly, and now looked quite moral and serious. As moral and serious, Wilbur thought, as only the immoral and frivolous can. 'No, I mean in spite of Chuck and the various extra expenses of the present, it's just that—well, things aren't the same now as they used to be, are they? A few years ago everything seemed so settled and peaceful, and all your entertaining and carrying on was part of that period. It seemed to belong to it. But now—everything's changing, isn't it? You see all these demonstrations every day now. And there are strikes the whole time now, and—oh, we're in difficult times Wilbur, and one has to be careful. Tighten the belt a little bit, you know. Make arrangements. In fact,' he said, lowering his voice and returning to his chair, 'I've been thinking quite seriously of leaving Rome, leaving Europe, recently. Because it *isn't* the same now as it was when we came, is it? When we first came here this was a sort of magic city. As if—oh, I don't know—as if *you'd* invented it, Wilbur. But there's an acrid smell in the air now, and it's nothing to do with the traffic. There's an underlying tension, a—I don't know what.'

'The rumble of the tumbril,' Wilbur murmured.

'Oh ha ha,' Jim shook perfunctorily. 'Yes. That's just it. And so you see, that's why I have to be a little bit careful. Because if I do move it's going to be a terrific upheaval, and—'

'And what?' the bad-breathed Chuck said, entering the room behind Jim. 'What are you talking about?'

'Oh heavens, I didn't hear you come in,' Jim said, obviously extremely pleased by this intrusion, which promised to cheer up what was getting to be an extremely trying session.

'About how expensive it would be if I decided to move from Rome.'

'Oh Jesus Christ,' Chuck snarled. 'You are so fucking cheap Jim.' He turned then to Wilbur, as if he were a friend, or an ally, and went on, 'Doesn't he make you sick? Here are we selling our souls, peddling our asses, grovelling in the dust to pick up the few odd coins that are tossed our way, and he's worrying about the expense of moving from one palace to another. My God, you make me puke Jim, you really do. Doesn't he make you puke, Wilbur?'

Wilbur forebore to give his opinion; and Jim, of course, staring delightedly at the tall, well built, ugly young man who was facing him with fury, simply—laughed.

'Oh really Chuck,' he trembled. 'How can you be so facile? And I was just telling Wilbur how intelligent you were. Oh heavens. Oh ha ha ha. Oh do get yourself a drink, or smoke one of your funny cigarettes. Oh, what a way to live. Oh ha ha ha ha ha. Oh ha ha ha.'

'I must be going I'm afraid, James,' Wilbur said.

Jim didn't make him puke. Nothing, ever again, would make him puke, Wilbur thought as he went back into his own tawdry, ridiculous apartment, that only a couple of hours ago had been so original and wonderful, and now looked like the backstage of a third-rate repertory company. Pam had hungered for a new life; Jim was frightened of the communists; what would Betty and Bernard's excuses be for denying him any further support—when and if he told them, or they discovered, that he wasn't a murderer? Oh no, nothing would ever make him puke again, or shock him; not even the idea, which came to him as he flopped down on his bed, that maybe Pam herself had told him she wanted her money back simply in order to taunt him; to tempt him to do what he hadn't done, but what everyone believed he had. Nothing was impossible any more....

That was true, he told himself next morning, but it wasn't true that he'd never be shocked again. Because after an almost sleepless night, which he had spent tossing in his bed, stroking and whispering to Philip, and thinking of what Jim had said about Rome being a magic city which he had invented—and he was right there, it was a magic city; a city of glorious appearance, of stunning façade; a city of glittering beauty, where most of even the poorest boys and girls, the most politically aware and the entirely uncommitted, masked the reality of their situation by dressing, always, in the latest fashion, whatever it was; a city where, indeed, fashion, appearance, façade *were* reality—he was woken at seven-thirty by the phone; and when he asked sleepily, crossly, who was calling, he was told to come immediately to the central police station.

Oh why, he asked.

He would be told when he arrived.

Had something happened?

Yes indeed.

What?

He'd be told when he arrived.

But was it something that concerned him?

Possibly. Or rather, yes. How quickly could he get there?

Immediately, Wilbur muttered, and putting the phone down, got out of bed.

But when he got to the police station half an hour later, he wasn't told at once what had happened. First of all he was shown into a grey painted office and sat down on a wooden chair and asked if he wanted a coffee.

Then, with the coffee in his hand, he was asked, in English, what he had done yesterday.

'I'm afraid I must ask you what all this is about,' Wilbur protested, 'before I answer your questions.'

Yes of course, the grey haired man in a grey business suit, who was sitting on the other side of a paper-covered table, and obviously enjoyed keeping people in suspense, said; and then repeated his question. What had Wilbur done yesterday?

Rome was a magic city; a dream city, where all—or most—that seemed, was. Rome was a nightmare city. And he had invented it. This was his nightmare he was in, Wilbur told himself, and only he had the power to wake himself from it; to wake up into the day. Except his power had deserted him, and he couldn't wake up. The nightmare was the day. He said he would like to speak to someone from the American Embassy.

'Yes of course,' the businessman/policeman said, 'though it's really not necessary. All we would like to know is—what did you do yesterday?'

'I got up at eight and went onto my terrace.'

He would try, at least, to be facetious.

But not even that worked. He was listened to with the most perfect courtesy.

'Then I went into my kitchen, had a coffee, and fed Philip, my cat. Then I took a bath, and went into my study and worked on a novel for two hours. Then I did some translating, of a film script. Then I prepared lunch, and ate it.'

'Alone?'

'No, with my secretary, and with a most charming girl whose father was the Bulgarian ambassador to the Holy See before the last war. She—'

'Were you with your secretary all morning?'

'Yes.'

'What time did your friend leave?'

'At three.'

'And your secretary?'

'At three, too.'

'And then?'

'I took a siesta for a couple of hours.'

'And then?'

'I took a taxi and went to have a drink with a very old friend of mine.'

'Whose name is?'

'James Simpson.'

'Who lives?'

'Just off Piazza Margana.'

'And how long did you stay with your friend?'

'An hour and a half maybe, two hours. I was home again at quarter to eight.'

'What did you talk about with Mr Simpson?'

'Oh good heavens,' Wilbur protested, sounding, he heard, very much like Jim himself.

'Did you ask him to lend you some money?'

Wilbur started to feel faint. Jim—or more probably Chuck—had, as an appalling joke, told the police that he had killed Pam....

'Yes,' he murmured weakly.

'Is Mr Simpson homosexual?'

'I don't—'

'He's a very old friend of yours.'

'Yes, he is.'

'And has he been living with a certain Mr Chuck Collins for the last few months?'

'Yes.'

'Did Mr Collins hear you ask Mr Simpson for money?'

'I don't know. Possibly.'

'Did you have a fight with Mr Simpson?'

'No.'

'Did Mr Collins?'

'No. Not while I was there.'

'Now tell me, Mr George. Did Mr Simpson make a ridiculous accusation that you were responsible for the death of a certain Mrs Pamela Winter?'

Wilbur closed his eyes, and didn't reply. He couldn't.

'Did he, Mr George?'

'No,' Wilbur barely whispered. 'This old friend of ours, Mrs Winter, died last August. Mr Simpson and I had a sort of—running joke between us that I had—'

'Killed her?'

Wilbur nodded.

'But it was only a joke between the two of you?'

'Yes,' Wilbur whispered.

'And never any more than a joke?'

'No,' Wilbur whispered.

'And Mr Collins never tried to blackmail you because of this joke—believing it to be more than a joke?'

'Good heavens no,' Wilbur said, quite strongly now. The idea that the unspeakable Chuck might even try to do such a thing had never occurred to him.

'And after you left Mr Simpson's, and went home, what did you do?'

'I rested briefly on my bed, and then had a quiet dinner party for two very old and dear friends from Alabama.'

'And what time did they leave?'

'About one o'clock.'

'And then?'

'I went to bed.'

'And after you left Mr Simpson, you had no further communication with him—or with Mr Collins?'

'No,' Wilbur said; and then, realizing that they had left the subject of Pam's death—which indeed this businessman playing the part of a policeman had defined as a 'ridiculous accusation'—and no longer fearing quite so much that he might be the victim of some practical joke, suddenly guessed—or suspected—what the grey haired man on the other side of the desk was driving at.

'Has something happened to Mr Collins?' he asked.

'To Mr Collins, no. He apparently left Mr Simpson's house shortly after you did and didn't return till two o'clock this morning. But to Mr Simpson, yes.'

'Oh no,' Wilbur breathed. 'What?'

'He's been murdered, Mr George. Murdered. Some time early this morning. And murdered in the most horrible—and peculiar—way. He was tortured, blinded, stabbed with a knitting needle, and then had his heart cut out. And then whoever killed him put his heart on the electric spit in his kitchen—and grilled it.'

'Oh no,' Wilbur gasped. 'Oh no. Oh no.' And then, suddenly, unable to control himself and completely hysterical, he burst into tears.

SEVEN

'The Ritual Murder', the papers called it; and though most of them differed in the actual rites involved, none of them erred on the side of understatement. They also, all of them, after giving their detailed descriptions of the various horrors that poor Jim had suffered, had separate stories by the side of the main articles, which were headed 'Black Magic?'

And Wilbur, as he sat barricaded in his home, refusing to answer his phone, or see anyone apart from Lillian—who came, at his request, to sleep on his living room sofa for four nights, as well as spending all her days with him—did nothing but read all these stories, and nod his head in a distracted way at those questioning headlines. Black Magic. Black Magic... What else could it be? Pam had refused him money, and she had died. Jim had refused him money; and he had died. And oh, the papers could talk about the American chain-store owner's predilection for delinquent boys, and say that undoubtedly it was at the hands of one of these that he had met his atrocious death—but he, Wilbur George, knew better. Well, maybe one of these boys—because it seemed the police didn't believe Chuck was responsible—had been the material agent, but that didn't mean much. For what dark angel had guided him in his madness; what evil spirit had possessed him, and inspired him to do what he had done?

Sure, the communist papers could say that it was the obscene spirit of capitalism that had possessed the doubtlessly underprivileged, undereducated, underdeveloped killer, and destroyed Jim; and the right-wing papers could say it was the dark angel of moral degeneracy, of perversion, of corroded values and permissiveness. But these were merely prosaic explanations. Rhetoric for the dull. But it wasn't the truth. It couldn't be. No, Wilbur told himself hour after hour as he read the papers mechanically, ate mechanically, slept mechanically, and even stroked the cat mechanically; the truth lay here, in this apartment; in this plump and pale heap of flesh that came from Carolina. The truth lay in the poetry of his life and world; in the life and world that he had invented. And it was from this apartment, this flesh, that the spirits and angels of death had flown out, to find a home in the rough and unsuspecting body of some Roman street-boy; a street-boy who even now must be hiding somewhere, frightened, horrified, staring at his dirty-nailed fingers, and wondering dumbly what it was that had made them clutch the knitting needles and plunge them into the old American; that had made them rip open that heaving chest and drag out the living heart, to impale it, so grotesquely, on an electric griddle. Even now some poor if you like, under-privileged if you like, degenerate, corrupted, perverted if you like, but some, certainly, helpless street-boy, was wondering: 'Why was I chosen?'

Why indeed, Wilbur asked the paintings on his wall, and the wood and silver and papier mâché monkeys. Why indeed? He wouldn't have had that boy chosen, whoever he was, for anything in the world. Yet he had been. He was the elected one. He had been made guilty....

Oh no, Wilbur said, time and time again to his winged and mirrored clocks, to his lacquered and inlaid musical boxes, and to his rows of Persian camel bells. 'Oh no,' he said out loud, with tears running down his face: 'don't let that boy be guilty. Don't let anyone be guilty. Let reality reverse itself and go back for a few days, and work itself out in a different way. Let it all be a dream. Oh don't let Jim be dead,' he cried. 'Oh please, oh please, don't let Jim be dead.'

'Hush,' Lillian said softly, and stroked the top of his head as he let it lie on his work table, soaking the pages of his novel. 'It's terrible, but tears won't bring him back. You must try to calm yourself. You can't go on like this.'
'I know,' Wilbur sobbed; and he did know.
'Would you like a brandy?'
'No thank you, dear child. I couldn't drink a thing.'

And he didn't drink a thing for four days; until he woke up that fourth morning too worn out to mourn any more, or even to struggle. All right, some insane youth whom Jim had picked up had murdered him in a fit of insanity. If that was the version the world wanted, that was the version the world could have.
And telling himself that, he got up, had a bath, and asked Lillian to put a shot of brandy in the coffee she was preparing for him.
'Oh I'm so glad, you're looking better this morning,' the girl lilted gently as she brought him the cup. 'I've been so worried these last few days. You know you've been having a real breakdown.'
'Yes, I know my dear. And I can't tell you how grateful I am to you for your help.'
'Oh, that's all right. In times like this we must all stick together.'
'Yes indeed. Yes indeed,' Wilbur said, and managed a faint smile. Oh if only she knew, he thought. If only she *knew.*
'And there's nothing anyone could have done.'
'I know,' he said—and thought, now; how wrong you are, dear child. There is something I could have done. I could have not released that spirit, not sent out— Stop it, he told himself. Stop it. Lillian was right. The papers were right. Even the radio, which had announced that morning on the news that a youth with a history of mental illness and

violence was being held for questioning in relation to Jim's death, was right. They were all right. There was no truth but the official truth; and there was nothing *anyone* could have done. It was sheer madness to think that he was in any way responsible. Of course he wasn't. It had just been the shock of Jim's death which had made him think that he was. A shock so great that, as Lillian had said, he had had a sort of breakdown. Now he was starting to get over it; and within a few days these absurd and horrifying feelings of guilt, these visions of dark angels, would have left him completely.

Or would they, he wondered wretchedly that afternoon as he opened the door to an unannounced and green-turbaned Betty. Because after she had excused herself for coming round without phoning first, and explained her coming by saying that she had been worried by his refusal to answer the phone, she looked at him gravely, as if searching for signs of—what?—and murmured, with studied, almost arch mournfulness, 'Oh Wilbur dear, there are dark angels abroad in the world nowadays, aren't there?'

Oh God, Wilbur thought, she too. I can't bear it. She, too, knows. Or if she doesn't know, she suspects. But then, as he had earlier, he said to himself, stop it. To Betty he said, 'Yes my dear. Though perhaps no more nowadays than there have always been.'

'Oh, do you think so?' She sounded unconvinced. 'Maybe you're right. But it just seems to me that before there was some sort of explanation for everything, however terrible. A historical or economic or something explanation. But now—oh, chaos seems so random.'

'Oh come now, Betty. Take off your coat my dear, and sit down. And let's not talk about—tragic events.'

'Oh no, let's not. Because really—'

But of course it was hard not to talk about them. They

hung over the afternoon like a dark cloud, and so dominated the silences—when they didn't dominate the conversation—that it was easier, finally, to give in and talk about nothing else.

'But why do you think a boy would do something like that,' Betty sighed. 'He must have been *possessed*.'

'Yes,' Wilbur agreed, 'he must have been.'

'If of course this one they're holding did it. They probably just picked on some poor mentally retarded youth whom it would be easy to pin the blame on. To satisfy public opinion. They'll probably never discover the real murderer.'

What did she mean....

'Well if this boy didn't do it, who do you think did?'

'Oh I don't know, my dear,' Betty said—and, strangely, laughed. 'As I say, we'll probably never know.'

'The police are fairly certain that it wasn't that person who's been living with Jim for the last few months.'

'I know. Tell me, what was he like?'

'Chuck? Oh, unspeakable. And quite capable of having killed Jim, I'm sure.'

Betty laughed again. 'We were all quite capable of that.' And then—narrowing her eyes slightly?—she said 'I read in one of the papers that you'd been to visit him that afternoon. They were reconstructing—you know, the last day in the life of.'

'I didn't see that,' Wilbur breathed. Just how much had been reconstructed? What details had the police given to the press? His asking for money? Jim's refusal? No, surely not. Yet it was possible. Perhaps Chuck had talked to some journalists, too; he would have loved to see his insinuations in print, knowing how humiliating they would be. But he didn't dare ask; and in any case, Betty would probably tell him, sooner or later. He said, 'But I did go, yes. That was all the more reason for it being such a shock. To see someone just hours before they're killed.'

'The police didn't suspect you'd done it, did they?'

'No. Good heavens no. At least,' Wilbur added, 'I don't think so.' That he might have been suspected of the actual crime—and not merely in some poetic way—had never occurred to him. And yet, he thought now, it should have done, with all those questions he had been asked. That it hadn't was probably due to the way that policeman had gotten—or not gotten—to the point; stringing out his questions without ever saying, until the end, that Jim was dead. Either that, or he had been so shocked, his collapse had been so sudden and so total when he *had* been told—and he had been so convinced that he was spiritually, as it were, responsible for the crime—that he hadn't been able to think that he might be held materially responsible as well.

'Though I guess they might have. My guests left here at one, and they estimated that Jim was killed at one-thirty.'

Betty smiled. 'I was quite alone myself at that hour.' She said it encouragingly; as if she hoped that her availability, too, for the crime, would prompt Wilbur on to further confessions of some nature....

And as she smiled, contentedly, towards the window and the cold raw January afternoon, Wilbur, who had felt wretched when she had arrived, believing that she, too, might subscribe to the theory of his having released evil spirits or some such thing, now, suddenly, felt absolutely amazed. Because—and he *was* getting slow—it all at once became clear to him that Betty didn't just think he had killed Jim poetically—but believed he had done it in actual fact. He felt so amazed—not stunned, or sickened, as he had been when he had realized that everyone had suspected him of Pam's death—that for a moment he couldn't speak, and all he could do, or wanted to do, was gape at Betty. She honestly believed that he, her old friend Wilbur, her court fool and magician, had murdered Jim Simpson. And not by giving him an amiable shove in his garden, but in the most foul and abominable way possible. What was most amazing of all, he told himself as he gaped at her sitting there, the corners of her mouth just twitching slightly, her eyelids trembling, her green wool dress pulled chastely over her knees, was that she not only didn't appear to mind about this new crime she believed he had committed, but actually approved of it. Was delighted by it, for all its foulness!

'Betty dear,' he finally gasped, unable to contain himself any longer, in spite of the fact that the words sounded almost hilarious to him now, 'you don't think I killed Jim too, do you?'

Oh why, he asked himself immediately he had said it, had he added that 'too'....

Not that it mattered; Betty didn't appear to have heard it, so taken was she with his question. Her eyes sparkled, her teeth flashed, her head shook; and then, leaning over and laying a gracious hand on his arm, she cooed, 'Well of course you did my dear. You don't have to pretend with your old Betty.' Then she lowered her voice confidentially. 'What's more my dear, I'm glad you did. Because I'll tell you something now I've never told anyone. I don't know if you've ever heard any stories about one of Jim's young friends?'

Wilbur nodded; not because he knew which young friend Betty was talking about, but simply as a sort of reflex action; he was too speechless to do anything else.

'Well dear, twenty-six years ago, when I came to Rome—two years before I met you—and as I say, this is something I've never told anyone; it's been too painful for me to even think about—I didn't come alone. And it wasn't Hubert I came with, either—we were already divorced by then. Nor any other husband or lover. No—well, you've met Richard and Sheila and Virginia—but you didn't know I had another son, did you? Tommy....' Betty's voice became veiled for a second, as if a white silk scarf had been languidly draped over it. 'He was the youngest, and—oh, he was so beautiful Wilbur. In every way. You'd have adored him. In fact I came to Rome because of him. Because I thought after he'd finished school we'd come to Europe together, and stay a year here, a year in Paris, and a year in London. To round him off, if you know what I mean. We didn't see anyone when we first arrived—just went everywhere together. The museums, churches, the opera—down to Sicily, to Florence, to Venice. And it was so wonderful to see things with Tommy. He had such enthusiasm, he could bring even the stalest view to life, reawake one's interest in even the most reproduced painting. Everything we saw—it was like seeing it for the first time with him. Even the sky in the morning—the flowers. Oh Wilbur, I remember when we first saw the Grand Canal together. It was a late afternoon in October, everything pale and gold and with that incredible transparent, violet light—and we stood on the Rialto for about half an hour, just soaking it in, until Tommy turned to me and whispered—as if we were alone there, which we *were* in a way—"Mother, I've just discovered the vein that leads to the perfect human heart." And oh, Wilbur, he was right. That was exactly it. One was looking at—oh dear, the very centre of perfection, the very heart of the entire human spirit.' Betty swallowed deeply. 'Anyway, after about six months here I thought that maybe we should see one or two people. I mean—we got on so well together it was wonderful. But I didn't want Tommy to risk getting bored—and besides, I thought that to meet some "characters" was all part of his education too. So I took him round to see some old countesses and people I'd known before the war, and a few of the more interesting foreign residents. One of these—though I'd never met her before, but had a letter of introduction to her—was Pam Winter. I didn't like her from the word go—I thought she was a venomous creature—but

Tommy was quite amused by her. I mean she did *look* very odd, and with that voice of hers and everything—and she fairly doted on him. It was almost obscene—she couldn't keep her hands off him. I think part of it was that she knew I didn't like her, and wanted to spite me. Anyway, one day she phoned and very pointedly asked Tommy to dinner and not me. Well I didn't care of course, and told him to go if he wanted to—which he did. And there, who should he meet—who had Pam *invited* him to meet—but Jim Simpson, who was passing through town. Jim of course fell madly in love with Tommy immediately, and the very next morning was calling to invite him here, there and everywhere, asking how long he was going to be in Rome, etc. At the time of course I didn't know Jim or what he was like. And I think Tommy was flattered by all his attention. Naturally, for a boy his age. However, after about a week, I told him to invite Jim over to the apartment where we were staying, and of course I got the picture right away. Well you know I've always been very liberal, and have always thought that everyone has the perfect right to do exactly what they like with their life, in every way. But I did think it was my duty to warn Tommy what he might be getting into. He said yes, he knew, so I told myself "Betty, don't be a jealous mother, and the experience won't hurt the boy." ' Betty closed her eyes dramatically now, and a spasm of something—pain?—passed over her smooth and stretched skin. 'But after a month Tommy came up to me one day and said, "Mother, I want to stay in Rome and take an apartment with Jim." That made my eyebrows shoot up, I can tell you. But I said, "Oh yes dear, why?" And do you know what he said? "Because I'm in love with him." Well, I'm afraid, with all my liberality, that really shocked me. Because—I mean—well—if Jim had been young and attractive or something. Or particularly intelligent. Or—*something*. But he was an uncultured forty-year-old man whose only purpose in life seemed to be spending money and seducing young boys. But I controlled myself and asked Tommy why he thought he was in love. And he said it was because he found there was a quality of fatality in Jim, a sense of despair that—and these were his exact words—rang deep and pure like a bell tolling from *une cathédrale engloutée*. I told him I didn't think that was a very good reason for falling in love with someone, nor did it promise well for the future of any relationship. But Tommy said he'd never heard a note so deep, and—well, he was attracted to it. Fatally attracted....' Betty shivered. 'So they set up house together, and I stayed on, trying to make the best of a bad situation. And for about six months it seemed I might be wrong. Tommy's love seemed to do wonders for Jim, made him lose weight, become more serious—everything. Probably because it was a unique experience for him. For not only had someone fallen in love with him, but here was someone who was young, beautiful, and couldn't possibly have any interest in his financial situation. It should have been perfect. But it was just this that—' Betty stopped for a second, gathering her forces for the final assault on her story. 'Jim was too corrupted. Too truly wicked. And having found what was, I say, in every respect an almost perfect relationship—couldn't cope with it. He longed to be humiliated, to be used, to be cheated. I'm not saying he didn't love Tommy himself. He did. But he hated him just because he did love him, and because Tommy loved him. Anyway, one night about three o'clock in the morning I got this hysterical phone call from Jim, telling me to come over immediately. I thought that perhaps he and Tommy had had a great fight. But when I arrived—Jim told me that indeed he and Tommy had had a fight earlier in the evening, as a result of which he had gone out to the cinema and then for a walk. He had come back in just a minute before he called me. And then he took me into the bedroom and—oh, Wilbur, it was the most appalling moment of my whole life. And I shall never, to the day I die, understand how Jim, however much he hated me, could have done such a thing to me, shown me such a thing. Because there, in a bedroom that was simply a lake of blood, was my Tommy—or all that was left of him. Because—oh Wilbur—my Tommy, my beautiful Tommy, had been killed and mutilated beyond recognition. There were pieces of him everywhere. Everywhere. And I remember that all I could do was say to Jim, "Have you called the police yet?" and when he told me no, go to the phone and say in the coldest possible way, "Will you please come immediately, there's been a murder." '

Some time passed before Wilbur dared break the silence, and whisper, 'Oh Betty.'

'I was cold like that for a week—through all the investigations and post-mortem and funeral—and then I went mad. Completely, utterly insane. I was taken to a clinic and kept there for six months. When I came out I heard that some boy had been arrested, charged with Tommy's murder, tried, found guilty, and sentenced to life imprisonment. But I know that Tommy didn't, couldn't have picked up any boy. It was Jim. It had to be Jim. It had to be Jim who had paid the boy—paid him lavishly I don't doubt—to do what he had done, and go to prison if necessary.' Betty gave a tiny smile. 'Of course he was released years ago, and is probably living in a villa in the south of France at this very moment with the money Jim gave him. And Jim did it just because he couldn't bear to love or be loved. I know it. When I came out of the clinic I thought for a while that as soon as I had my strength back I would leave Rome, and try to pick up some sort of life again. But just as I was getting ready to—I met you, Wilbur dear. And you—of course you didn't know what I'd been through, and nor did anyone else, because with a great deal of bribes we were able to keep everything out of the papers, and when people asked I said Tommy had gone back to America. But you gave me strength, my dear, to live again. Because you had that same magic quality that Tommy had—that way of bringing even the most inanimate object to life with a word, or a gesture. No, you didn't know it, but you taught me how to live again. You gave me back my faith in life. In the *magic* of life. And for this I shall be eternally grateful. Eternally grateful. And as soon as I met you I knew, too, that through your—magic powers, one day I would have my revenge on Jim Simpson. On Jim, and on Pam. And then when first Pam—and then the other day, when I read in the paper what had happened to Jim—well, I *knew*. I knew that you had done it for me. Done it without knowing my story, done it for reasons of your own. But it was all so perfect, only you could have done it. Only an artist could have managed such symmetry, drawn such a perfect parabola. Oh Wilbur dear—thank you. Thank you for everything. And now', Betty said, suddenly standing up and gazing bravely towards the cold grey window pane, 'if you'll excuse me dear, I must go. I'm a little upset. And you must be, too, after all this. In fact dear, if you don't mind, tomorrow I think I shall whisk you off to the country, and we'll just sit round the fire together for a week, and eat chestnuts and be kind to each other.' She looked at him urgently. 'You will come dear, won't you? Please. We both need it. Say you'll come.'

Obediently, but with a lump in his throat—and still sitting down—Wilbur murmured, 'Of course I'll come, my dear.'

How could he have refused? . . .

'Oh thank you my love. I'll call tomorrow morning, and we'll set off after lunch. All right?'

'All right,' Wilbur whispered.

'And don't you move. I can let myself out. And—' and then Betty leaned over and kissed him—'God bless you.'

When she got to the door she turned and said, 'Oh, and do you know what Jim did when I came out of the clinic? I guess he was trying to convince himself that he wasn't guilty. He wrote me a letter saying it was all my fault what had happened. That I had always tried to come between him and Tommy, and they had had that fight that night because of me. Because Tommy wanted to come back to me. He even said that it was because of me, because I had kept Tommy away from the real, sordid world, kept him away so much that he longed for it, that Tommy had betrayed him—betrayed him!—and had gone out searching for the boy who would kill him. Can you imagine. Can you *imagine*?'

Wilbur, as he sat in his chair for an hour or so after Betty had left, could imagine anything at this point. But he went on sitting, without moving, because he was too weak to move. Too weak to do anything but tell himself that Betty believed he had murdered Jim, that tomorrow Betty was going to take him off to the country for a week—and he had no choice but to go; he was no longer the court fool, but the slave; a will-less, right-less slave—and above all, too weak to do anything but repeat to himself over and over again that though Betty's story had been gripping, and horrifying, and convincing in every detail—he didn't believe a word of it. Not one word....

It was dark before he did move, and in spite of the heating, he was very cold. He was rigid with cold; and even after he had stumbled across the room and switched on a lamp—how dull the bulb was; how gloomy the light that illuminated his lifetime's collection of toys, and tack—poured himself a whisky, drunk it neat, then gone into the bathroom and had a hot bath, he was still cold. As cold as the grave....

Wrapped in sweaters and a heavy woollen jacket, he went into his study and started to work on his novel. It was the only thing he could do, he thought, as he reeled from page to page, his freezing hand clutching the pen as desperately as Pam had clutched her stick. The only possible thing; to create, and lose himself in another world. Because this world, the world he had created and lived in and functioned so well in for so long, had suddenly gone spinning off its axis; gone wildly, crazily out of control. Of course, he muttered to the wall in front of him, he would have liked to call someone, and talk to them, but if he did, he knew it would be Bernard he would call. Just to hear him, too, say that it was a damn good thing he had done, killing Jim Simpson; just to hear him, too, make up some story that justified this attitude. And for the moment he couldn't face that. So he called no one, and stayed on in his study, writing and writing, until his teeth were chattering and his hand shaking so much that he couldn't continue.

Then, clutching Philip to him to get, maybe, some warmth from him—and in fact the cat, after a while, began to succeed where radiators, whisky and baths had failed—he went, slowly, to bed.

He was unable to call anyone the following morning, too—unable, that is, to call Bernard—and told Lillian that he was only at home to Betty. And having spoken to her and agreed to be ready to be collected at two, and having asked Lillian if she would stay in the apartment to look after Philip—of course with her Chinese friend, if she and he wanted—and having decided that he had too much to do to be able to settle down and write, he simply spent the morning pottering around, doing nothing; and realizing that he felt, for the first time in his life, extraordinarily lonely. And it wasn't at all a pleasant feeling. Rather it was terrible, and frightening. Lonely. Exiled ... To be cut off from the world. To be deported, alone, to an unknown country. To a country one had had no hand in the making of. To a country where one was condemned to live with a word tattooed, however unjustly, on one's forehead. 'Murderer'....

EIGHT

Betty's house in the country was on the Argentario, a mile or two from Porto Ercole; a small, warm, comfortable house set in the middle of fifteen acres of olive groves and vineyards, overlooked by the wooded, iron-filled mountains, and near enough to the sea for the smell of it to come drifting through the cypresses and pines—when the wind was in the right direction. In the summer, if Betty was there, and often if she wasn't, it was filled with people trailing their way to the swimming pool, all looking determinedly happy beneath their sun-tans, as if holidays alone in the year called for good nature and smiles. But in the winter there was never anyone there apart, occasionally, from Betty, and this was normally the time that Wilbur, when he went up to spend a weekend, enjoyed the most. He preferred the swimming pool when it was empty, and full of leaves; and he preferred the sound of the wind shaking the shutters, to the voices of sun-drunk people insisting on the good time they were having.

Normally....

This time, this bleak January, he did not enjoy himself. Because, and in spite of the determined—too determined—efforts of Betty, he still felt lonely, and it was still too new and unsettling a feeling for him to relax with it for a second. *He*, lonely; but he couldn't be, he told himself as he gazed disconsolately from his bedroom window in the morning. He *couldn't* be, he told himself as he walked up the narrow lanes above Betty's property, catching a glimpse every now and then of the grey sea and the boat-bobbing port. How they must rattle and ache in the wind, he thought, those boats that hadn't been hauled in for the winter. How they must click, and creak, and be conscious of all their cold spars, empty masts, and tarpaulin covered decks. How unused they must feel. How lonely....

He had never been able to conceive of the idea of loneliness before; had always considered it something that the constitutionally bleak and the champions of self-pity chose for themselves. He had never believed it could be forced on one. Yet obviously it could, he told himself as he went, alone, to bed at night. Oh, how it could.

Betty of course was aware that there was something wrong with him; but she, he was sure, put it down to remorse, or the after-effects of his efforts with Jim. She probably believed that murder, like any too heady a brew, gave one a hangover....

On the other hand, she treated the symptoms of his malaise as if she had known he were lonely. She insisted that they *do* something every day; either go for a walk, or go to visit those few friends of hers who lived in this part of the world all the year round, or go to lunch or dinner in some empty restaurant, which she would attempt to fill with laughs and jokes and stories. Once she even made him drive with her to Orbetello, and there go to some dismal comic movie that made her shriek. But all Wilbur could do was picture the road they had driven along to get there; a straight wet road running across the middle of the lagoon that separated the Argentario from the mainland; a straight wet road watched over by grey flightless sea-gulls, and telegraph poles sticking out of the water at crazy angles—as if at any second they might keel over, and interrupt for ever the fragile messages they carried.

Worst of all, Betty would not allow him to work on his book. She was quite shocked when he told her that he had started, after all these years, on a novel; in spite of the fact that she had, ostensibly, always lent him money just so he could.

'No Wilbur, I insist,' she said gently, with a dazzling smile, when he pleaded to be allowed to go up to his room. 'You're not yourself, and sitting up there all alone with only your thoughts is absolutely the least indicated thing to do. No. I won't hear of it. You can work when you go back to Rome if you must, but while you're here—no. You must relax, and be happy. And I don't want to hear another word on the subject. Now get us both a drink, dear, and come here and sit by the fire.'

The thing was, Wilbur knew, that only if he had been allowed to work could he have escaped from his loneliness; sitting at his table, making the imaginary real; or perhaps the real, imaginary....

How he longed to; to escape into that world of living, breathing people; where people talked, and touched, did and died; into that world where people sat around fires in houses in the country, and longed to be somewhere else.

But he was too weak, too worn out to argue. Besides, he was no longer free, no longer the fool who could fly where he would at will. Now he was the slave, the guilty slave, who, up in the Big House, depended on the Master's—or in this case, Mistress's—whim.

And the Mistress wished him to be with her, and talk; talk frankly, *seriously*, as they had never talked before; with earnestness, and eyes meeting meaningfully.

'Oh do tell me Wilbur, have you ever been in love,' Betty asked him one evening as she kept him cornered in a big beige sofa.

'I've always been in love,' Wilbur tried. 'All my life.'

But there was no evading the all powerful Betty, who raised a golden, bat-sleeved arm and tapped him playfully on the knee.

'Yes I know you have. But I mean—with people.'

'Yes my dear. With people, cats, flowers, monkeys, books, pictures, food, clouds—'

'Wilbur, you're teasing me. With any *particular* people.'

Various images came to Wilbur for a second; images of faces from the past. Pale faces, with red voracious mouths like those of young birds. Dark faces, with black hair and pink tongues. Long faces, round faces. Funny faces, frowning faces, beautiful faces....

'No, my dear, never,' he said. 'Oh, I've had my infatuations and my periods of depravity, but love of any one particular person has always seemed such a limitation. It excludes too much, it seems to me.'

Why hadn't he kept his mouth shut?...

'Oh but you're wrong. It can include *everything* if it's with the right person.'

'Then I've obviously never met the right person.'

'Oh my dear, and you've never felt lonely?'

'No, never for an instant,' Wilbur said. 'Good God, there's so much in the world, how could I? How can anyone?'

'But so few of us, if any, have your talent for filling the world.'

'Well maybe that's it, my dear. And while we're talking of filling, my glass is empty. But I must say,' he added, as he attempted to edge his way out of the sofa—though Betty would have none of it, and waved him down as she stretched behind her for the whisky—'I've never ever understood the meaning of the word loneliness.'

Until now, was the obvious if unnecessary retort to this statement, Wilbur thought. But though it was unnecessary, he couldn't help saying it to himself. And saying it, furthermore, with such bitterness that he once more had an image of all those faces from the past—those pale faces, dark faces, frowning faces and beautiful faces—as they pleaded with him, shouted at him, begged him, insulted him; all trying to stop him making light of their feelings; all trying to stop him being a fool; all trying to make him answer in the affirmative their questions: 'Don't you understand what I'm talking about?' 'Don't you know the meaning of the word love?' And finally, as a last resort, 'But haven't you ever been lonely, Wilbur?'

No, no, and no, he remembered himself saying....

Another evening Betty said, 'Do tell me about your childhood, dear.'

'Oh Betty, I've told you a hundred times.'

'Yes, I know. But I hate seeing you unhappy like this, and sometimes, if we talk about our childhood—I don't know. It makes things better. Besides,' she laughed, the steel creeping into her voice, 'every time you've told me you've told me something different.'

'That's because I had so many different childhoods.'

'Well, tell me the truth tonight. The real one.'

'My dear, they're all real.'

'They can't be.'

'Well they are.'

He heard he sounded sulky, and wondered whether such insolence would be allowed to pass.

It wasn't.

'No,' Betty cried, 'I won't stand for that. Come along now. You were born in South Carolina, and orphaned at the age of one—'

That was one of the constants in his stories. How he had been orphaned tended to vary slightly, according to his listener. His parents, young, bright and thoughtless, the original flappers and party-goers, had killed themselves by driving their car off the road while drunk on champagne. Or: his mother had been a bar-girl, his father an alcoholic; they had been knocked down and killed by a car while standing in the middle of the road, brawling. Or: his parents, youthful and intense, had been two of the earliest civil-rights workers. While driving down a dark country road at night they had been ambushed and shot by the Ku-Klux-Klan. Their death had been put down as 'due to drunken driving'. The final version of his parents' death—that he only occasionally gave—was that his mother, a white Russian who had arrived in the States just before or just after the Revolution, had decided that life was at least as bad as, if not worse, in this free America than it had been or was in the Russia she had fled from, and unable to bear the idea of watching her baby being slowly corrupted, had decided to kill herself by driving into a brick wall. She had taken her husband, who was American and already beyond hope, with her; but she had spared the child on the theory that maybe, just maybe, he would be strong enough, or intelligent enough, or something enough, to save himself.

Another constant of his stories was that he had no, absolutely no relations to whom to be entrusted after his parents' death—which also explained in part the conflicting accounts of those parents and their deaths. After all—how could mere strangers be relied upon to tell him, when he was twelve years old, what had *really* happened? Or even old newspaper reports, if they could have been found?

He wasn't sent to an orphanage however, or an institution. Various people who had known his parents took pity on the one-year-old child, and felt it their duty to give him a home. These people were—again, according to the listener—a thirty-year-old British bachelor, the *de rigueur* Englishman to be found in every town in the world, who was the youngest son or the blackest sheep of some fairly noble family from Suffolk called Winter—('Oh Pamela, I know he has to be a relation. Somewhere. Somehow.')—who adopted the baby for reasons, apart from those of pity and duty, it was better not to go into; an extremely old lady, Miss Viola Bartlett, who lived in a white Southern mansion and who just *adored* marionettes and dolls, and wasn't too fussy whether they were living or merely made of papier-mâché; a young married couple, painters, who were from New England but had come south for the colour (*her* name, before her marriage, had been Dale); and two spinsters, Miss Annie and Miss Rachel, who, whilst *quite* against marriage to men, would have liked, had it been possible, to have offspring of their own. (Miss Annie was always Miss Annie to everyone; but really she was Miss Amy. Miss Amy Simpson....)

The third and last constant of Wilbur's stories of his childhood was that none of these various surrogate parents gave him much in the way of a formal education, but all of them gave him what was far more precious; a sense of scope, and space; a sense of interior worlds, and magic. They also instilled in him the sense that hospitality—their hospitality in particular, but all hospitality in general—was the most sacred of all virtues, and gave him a taste for flight.

He fled, accordingly, at the age of sixteen; to New York. Or at the age of seventeen. Or to Paris, at the age of eighteen....

This evening he gave Betty a mixture of all these stories—a mixture he hoped she hadn't heard before. Feeling mean, however he obstinately referred to the old lady in the white Southern mansion simply as Miss Viola; thus depriving Betty, whose maiden name had been Bartlett, of the chance to exclaim as she had so often in the past, 'Oh that *is* extraordinary, isn't it Wilbur? And though I've never heard of a Bartlett in South Carolina, there are so many of us all over the South that I just know she must be a great-aunt or something. I love to think so, anyway. It makes me feel we've been in touch all our lives, and that we were bound to meet sooner or later. Oh I do so believe in the hidden links.'

What he did say was 'There now, my dear. And that's the truth. Every word of it.'

'Oh Wilbur, you're impossible,' Betty cried. Then—to get her own back on him for his having omitted Miss Viola's last name, or because she felt it of a melancholy suitable to Wilbur's mood—she added softly, 'Though I must say, in spite of the way you make it all sound so magical, it must have been a very lonely childhood.'

'Lonely?' Wilbur said. 'Oh no, my dear. Never.'

But at the end of six days—and Wilbur still wasn't sure how long he was going to be kept up here; 'Oh, at least another day or two,' Betty murmured airily when he asked how long she could put off her return to the big city—his hostess had given up the attempt to distract him or amuse him, and seemed, even, to become preoccupied and anxious herself. So much so, in fact, that the night of that sixth day, as they sat nursing what would probably be their final brandies before going to bed, and after an evening in which she had done nothing but repeat, almost word for word, what Wilbur himself had said ('That is a charming painting, Betty, really.' 'Oh yes, Wilbur, it *is* a charming painting.' 'My dear, this wine is extraordinary.' 'Yes, it is an extraordinary wine, isn't it?'), Betty started talking again about what had happened to her son, and about Jim's—and Pam's—responsibility for the tragedy.

'What's over is over, Betty dear,' Wilbur tried to soothe her with. 'What's done is done.'

'But it isn't all over,' Betty frowned, and attempted a brave smile. 'Things like that never are, are they, dear?'

'Oh I don't know. I mean we can come to terms with even the most terrible facts of life.'

'Yes, I know,' Betty sighed, running her finger round the top of her glass, and obviously trying to strike just the right note. 'But—there was one other thing I didn't tell you last week. One last little piece in the puzzle. One last little—turn of the screw.'

How the firelight flickered. How the rough, white, rustic walls showed all their cracks and pores. How the brandy in the glasses glowed, and how quiet the night outside was. No wind, no rain. No dogs barking, no bats squeaking. Just the deep, silent cold. The black, freezing January night....

'Bernard.'

It was one word, tossed out into the soft, warm room. And Betty didn't raise her head from her glass as she said it. She hardly moved her lips.

'Bernard Dale.'

Then she was silent for a while, letting the name spread out, fall, cover the room like a white cloth being spread over furniture by someone who is leaving a house for ever.

And she need, in fact, have said nothing more. Wilbur could have finished her speech for her. But there were certain rules to be obeyed; a certain formality to be observed. One had to lock the front door, even if one was never returning.

'In a way it's he, even more than Pam or Jim, whom I blame for what happened.' Once more Betty paused; before launching into her story proper. 'I had known Bernard in New York, before I came here. He and Hubert had done business together on various occasions. I never liked him, even then. He was always a cruel, prejudiced man. And the way he treated his wife—he crushed her out of existence. Literally. She just got smaller and smaller, more and more withered. And she'd been a pretty little thing. But—well, that's nothing to do with me. Anyway, Tommy became friendly with Bernard's youngest, Arthur. They were at school together briefly, and, as I say, Hubert and Bernard met occasionally. He was a nice boy, but he took after his mother, and Bernard despised him for it, and was always trying to make him go out huntin' and shootin' and fishin'. You know that absurd, immature Hemingway complex that so many American men had at the time. Perhaps they still do. I wouldn't know.' Betty sighed. 'Well, Bernard didn't approve of Tommy's friendship with Arthur, but one summer—they were both just turned seventeen—Tommy asked me if he and Arthur could go and stay at a place we had in Maine. I was going to Europe, I don't know what Hubert was doing, so I said yes, of course. So off they went, and I flew off to Nice, where I was staying with a friend of mine. I'd been there about two weeks when suddenly, who should turn up at the door, but Tommy. He looked very pale and sick, and said that he and Arthur had had some sort of fight, and that—well, just that he preferred to spend the summer with me in the South of France. However, a week later it all came out. It appeared that he and Arthur had been getting on fine together. But then one evening, after they'd been there a few days, Bernard suddenly arrived, roaring drunk. He started screaming that he didn't want the two of them to be together, and that Tommy was corrupting Arthur or some such rubbish, and that they should both come with him. He took them to some cheap motel, told them it was time they both "had a woman", and more or less marched them into this room where he had paid some prostitute to wait. But she wasn't just an ordinary prostitute, Tommy told me. If she was a real prostitute at all. Because she was about fifty years old, fat and hideously ugly, and to cap it all, mentally retarded. And there he forced Arthur—at *gun*-point—to make love to this poor creature. Apparently it was the most hideous scene you can imagine. There was Bernard, drunk and screaming with laughter, and this wretched woman who was terrified and whimpering, and these two seventeen-year-old boys. Can you imagine, Wilbur? Seventeen. But anyway, Tommy told me, Arthur went with her. And then Bernard ordered Tommy to, too. But do you know what Tommy did? He said he suddenly felt terrifically calm, looked Bernard straight in the eye, and said, "no, and you can shoot me if you like." And then he went over to the bed and very gently soothed the poor woman who was lying there crying, told her to get dressed, and asked if she needed a ride home. He felt *so* calm, he said, that Bernard, like all bullies when someone stands up to them, was speechless, and didn't do a thing. And then Tommy picked up Bernard's car keys that were lying on a table, and took the woman out. But as he was leaving, do you know what he did? He stopped in front of Bernard, smiled at him, whispered, "I pity you," and then—you won't believe this Wilbur, but Tommy swore it was true; he said he *did* suddenly feel overcome with pity for Bernard—he leaned forward, and kissed Bernard right on the lips.

'And then, leaving Bernard and Arthur stranded, he drove the woman home—though he didn't know how to drive—and then, either by accident or design, crashed the car. And then he came back to New York, was sick for a week, phoned Arthur to make sure he was all right, and then got on a plane and came to Nice.'

Betty raised her head at last, and gazed, quiveringly, into the fire. She had tears in her eyes.

'Can you imagine, Wilbur,' she said again. 'Can you imagine doing that to two seventeen-year-old boys? And I'm convinced that that was why Tommy, later, had this thing about Jim. Because even though he told me about it, he was never able to laugh about it as he did about everything else, and obviously deep down he was so traumatized that when he met Jim, I'm sure he saw in him a combination of both Bernard and in a way, that prostitute. He was trying to exorcize his demons. What's more,' and now the tear-glittering eyes were closed, 'he would have succeeded. Or perhaps he had succeeded. I don't know. Maybe that was why Jim had him killed. But I do know that if it hadn't been for Bernard, Tommy would never have'—a wince—'fallen in love with Jim, and he'd still be alive today.'

A long, long pause; the highest, softest note spun out in the silent room. And then the final swoop, with a bend of the body, a clinching of the fist, the searchingest, deepest stare, and the faintest tremble of a smile on the pain-racked mouth.

'Oh Wilbur dear, work your magic for me just once more. Won't you? Please? For me. And then—well, now I've got all the trust fund business sorted out, and the children are all taken care of, I've got far more money than I need. And then the two of us—oh Wilbur, we could have such fun. Go everywhere, see everything. And you'll never have any more problems. And I know how difficult things are for you sometimes. But that's all over now. Just a serene old age, and happiness, and—oh Wilbur—you will do it for me, won't you? Work your magic one more time. Just one last time, for Betty. Say you will my dear. Please. Say you will.'

But Wilbur said nothing, and simply smiled at Betty for a while as he held her hand—and then turned his eyes towards the fire, and let the scented olive wood flare up and burn in his brain.

Bernard, three days later on the phone, was, as ever, altogether blunter.

'Jesus Christ, you're getting dangerous. That's two gone now, and one to go.'

'Oh Bernard, you old fool,' Wilbur said, playing the part of the Wilbur of old, but now feeling sick as he did so. *Why* had he lied about Pam, he asked himself. To Bernard, of all people; the one person he could, in the final analysis, have relied on if he had to. Because now, of course—

'As soon as I heard on the radio that someone had had their heart stuck on a spit, I thought that sounds like Wilbur's touch. And then when I heard it was Simpson, I knew it. Christ Almighty. You're a fucking maniac.'

'Oh Bernard, you know perfectly well I didn't do it.'

It was a plea from the heart.

'Of course you did. Don't *you* start getting a guilty conscience.'

'Oh Bernard—'

'And stop "oh Bernarding" me. If there's one thing I can't stand it's repentance. You're not repenting are you?'

'No, of course not. Why should I repent?'

'Well that's a relief. Where the hell have you been for the last two weeks. That Irish answering service of yours was all evasive every time I called, and just said, "Wilbur's not in," or "Wilbur's in the country." What were you doing? Lying low?'

'No. For the first four days after—what happened—I didn't feel like speaking to anyone. And then I was in the country.'

'At this time of year?'

'I'm trying to get on with my novel.'

'Oh novel crap. You know you haven't written a word for years.'

'Well I'm trying to now. Insurance for my old age.'

'Oh balls. I'm going to have to be your insurance for your old age, otherwise I'll go the way that Winter woman and Simpson went. By the way, how are you for money? Not seeing blood in front of your eyes for want of cash, are you?'

'I'm quite all right for the moment, thank you.'

He had found a cheque for a thousand dollars tucked in the pocket of his jacket when Betty had dropped him off outside his apartment yesterday evening....

'Just as well. But I'll tell you one thing, Wilbur George, you're not getting any promises of permanent support until you've done away with Madam Betty.'

'Oh Bernard—'

'I'm serious. You can't stop now. You've rid the world of two of its major scourges, and now there's only one left. And she's the worst of the three.'

'Oh, you're an impossible old fool.'

'And you're a fucking maniac. I always knew it though. What are you doing for dinner tonight?'

'Nothing.'

'Then come and eat with me, and we can work out the plan together.' A gruff old chuckle. 'Jesus, you've made me feel quite young again. What do you want to eat? I'll make you something special.'

'Heart,' Wilbur said, in spite of himself; and couldn't—also in spite of himself—keep a smile off his lips. Oh God, he thought, perhaps I really am going mad, if I'm starting to enjoy this nightmare. Starting to laugh at it all, as if it weren't serious any more.

But though it was all just as serious, just as much of a nightmare as ever, and though he *still* could see nothing funny about murder, he couldn't help enjoying himself that evening with Bernard. Just as he had enjoyed himself when he had come to see Bernard after Pam's death. That dark, gloomy apartment did something to his sense of balance. He couldn't help laughing....

Because as he had said on the phone, Bernard had never seemed so young and cheerful; so full of school-boyish enthusiasm. His little white hands tugged at his beard; his big cardigan-covered belly shook continually with spasms of mirth.

'Poison,' he said over the port. 'That's what's most suitable for Betty. A nice fantastic Southern potion, mixed in a mint julep.'

'Oh Bernard—'

'Poison for the poisonous.'

'What do you have against poor Betty?'

'Poor Betty my ass. That hag has done more damage in this world than the atom bomb.'

'You're exaggerating.'

'No I'm not. Jesus Christ. I don't know if I ever told you

this, but her youngest—who came to a nasty end, rumour has it—and my youngest were friends once, when they were kids. One year when they had just turned eighteen Madam Betty took them off for the summer to some darlin' ole mansion down in your part of the world—Louisiana. I was driving down to Florida for some reason, so I thought I'd call in and see them, unannounced. I arrived one evening at about nine, and do you know what I found? Your dear Betty dressed as a man, with blackface on, my Arthur wearing a confederate uniform, and her son and heir dressed as an ante-bellum Southern lady, with an old gown that woman kept in her attic for her "charades", she called them.'

'Oh Betty's such a mad creature,' Wilbur laughed.

'You're damn right she's mad. Not only had she dressed up two eighteen-year-old boys, and herself as a slave, but they were all high on cocaine. A great silver tray full of the stuff there was, and Madam saying, "Oh Bernard dear, have a sniff yourself." I dragged young Arthur off immediately, I can tell you, but we had problems with drugs for five years after that. She might have killed the boy, or turned him into an addict for life, if he hadn't had such a strong character and been able to kick the habit. Jesus!'

'How is he now?'

'Arthur? Oh, he's all right. Or no worse than any of my others. Married, with five milk-fed children.'

'I'm sure you're exaggerating, anyway,' Wilbur said; who could no more believe Bernard than he had been able to believe Betty herself. Perhaps, somewhere, there was a grain of truth in their stories, just as there was in his own, of his childhood, but—no, they couldn't be trusted, either of them. Perhaps, he thought, it was his own influence on the two of them. Two people who had come under his spell; had been touched by his magic....

'Of course I'm not exaggerating. You ask Arthur if you don't believe me. Or rather, don't, even if you could, because that's all a part of his life he tried to forget. He won't have the name of Betty Bartlett mentioned anywhere in the state of California. And also that's not a half of what she's done. I'd like to know how many other people she sacrificed on the Southern gothic altar of her craziness before the States got too hot for her and she fled here. Her first husband, for instance —the one she got the loot from. And I'd like to know what did happen to that boy of hers. Tommy, I think his name was. He probably tried to rebel against Momma, and she had him locked up in a mad-house. That's what I heard, anyway. He was involved in something very unpleasant, and the only way to save him from the gas chamber was by having him put away. He's probably still locked up, drugged to the eye-balls and swishing around pretending he's Scarlett O'Hara. No Wilbur, it's time she was stopped, and poison's the answer. Why don't you make a dinner for her, and slip something in the spare-ribs? *I'll* come if you do, and even eat some of that filthy Southern stuff you serve.'

'Filthy it is not.'

'Well I'll go so far as to say that it's great if it'll mean the end of Betty,' Bernard said. And then, carried away now by a real fit of laughter, and taking off his spectacles to wipe his eyes, he cackled, 'Jesus, I'd love to see it. Why don't you do it?'

'Oh Bernard,' Wilbur protested.

'If you don't, you won't get another cent from me,' the old man jeered. 'Or I'll go even further, and tell the police what you've done so far. Good God, yes, I think I shall blackmail you Wilbur! If you don't do away with the Bartlett woman, I shall tell the whole world what a fucking maniac you are. Jesus Christ, I swear I will,' he chuckled.

And, Wilbur thought, out of a sense of rumbustious fun, Bernard would be capable of doing that. He'd do it as a joke of course, but nevertheless....

* * *

Before he went home that night he also managed to get out of Bernard his reasons, or his ostentible reasons, for hating Pam and Jim.

Pam, according to Bernard, on the excuse that she—at the age of sixty—wanted the man herself, had come between 'a very good friend of mine' who was in love with Bobbie, and Bobbie—who was also in love with the man. In fact, for this friend—a fine person, a widower, who had been a real saint with his sickly, neurotic wife—and the tall fair English girl it had been the great love of their lives. But Pam, with lies and fabrications and falsehoods, had managed to so dirty and destroy their love, that eventually neither of the two could face it any longer, and Bobbie had fled to Australia, and the widower been condemned to a life-time of emptiness and regrets. 'And I'm not a sentimental man, Wilbur, but I can tell you. What that woman did ...'

Jim's crime—as Bernard told it—was of a different nature. 'Jesus Christ,' the bearded old man said, 'anyone can tell you I'm not a communist. But sometimes I think that the reds have their points. Because I got involved in some business dealings that jolly old Jim was making in the thirties, when he was a young man. And I can tell you Wilbur George, that your friend Simpson's fortune was made—or at least multiplied—by a series of the most dishonest, crookedest dealings I've ever come across in my life. And I'm as fond of an honest crook as anyone else, but there was nothing honest about Jim Simpson. He seemed to take delight in any transaction that would actively hurt people. That would split up families, cause strikers to be shot, widows thrown out into the streets, innocent people intimidated and maimed. He was the worst sort of gangster; the type who sits in his office while other people do his dirty work for him, and who proclaims himself a liberal because he doesn't mind associating with all the most violent thugs in town—in his bed. No Wilbur, he had it coming to him, and I'm glad, I'm really glad he got it.'

However, if Wilbur listened to all this in silence, and if, in the course of the evening, he did laugh with Bernard, when he came out into the street afterwards—again, exactly as had happened before when he had told Bernard how he had killed Pam—he was struck once more by the mess he had got himself into, and how very unfunny it was.

And it was so absurd, he told himself as he pulled his black coat around him and started to walk slowly home through the cold, narrow, deserted streets. It was absolutely absurd. All he had to do was say 'stop it'. To Betty. To Bernard. And to himself. To say stop it, and then resume his old life. And of course neither Betty nor Bernard could do anything—apart, maybe, from not give him any more money. But at this stage he didn't even care about that any more. He could always find some way of making ends meet, and if he couldn't—well, he would just have to tighten his belt a little. He didn't like the idea of course, but anything was better than this ridiculous nightmare. Anyway, even if after a period, they would probably go on helping him just as they always had. They were both of them just a bit mad at the moment, their heads turned by the deaths of Pam and Jim—deaths that had produced and released these fantasies they had recounted about each other, whose origins probably lay in some banal and trivial squabble they had let get out of hand, and had never bothered to settle with a simple phone-call or postcard. Yes, he thought, that was surely the explanation. They both felt ashamed of themselves for having been divided for so long by something stupid and petty, and now that it was too late to make amends to the dead, thought to justify themselves by making up these wild, melodramatic stories. That had to be the explanation—even of Bernard's animosity towards Betty, who was still alive, and vice versa. Because they had obviously, long ago, been friendly, if not actual friends. And now that they were both old, and with the deaths of Pam and Jim before them, they couldn't face admitting that their quarrel, too, was trivial; that they had been separated for all this time simply by pettiness, prejudice, and pride. For if they had admitted that, it would have meant admitting that their other quarrels, which they could no longer make up, had been ridiculous. So it was easier for them to lump the living with the dead, pretend, to themselves and to him, that there had been unforgivable wickednesses in the past, and hope that death would carry the other off before the cat got out of the bag, and revealed itself to be, indeed, just a cat, and not a four-headed, blood-stained monster.

They were getting old....

Me too, Wilbur thought, as the January wind made his cheeks sting and something in his back suddenly ache. Old and foolish. With all my talk of magic and nonsense, with all my silly dreams. I might bring out the best in people at times, but at other times I bring out the worst. And recently, with Betty and Bernard in particular, these have been other times. But now, really, is the time to say stop, to sober up and put an end to all this. And I shall. I shall. Because while there is nothing funny—and not only is murder not funny, nor is the spectacle of three people, who should know better, making idiots of themselves—there is, really, no nightmare either. We have all just been slightly mad for the last few months, and me more than anyone.

We're all just getting old....

That night, for the first time perhaps since last August, Wilbur slept not only for a long time, but also well; and when he woke he felt far better than he had for a long time. He felt, in fact, not only as sober as he had last night after leaving Bernard's, but also relaxed and immensely relieved, as if he had, more than having survived just the doubts and difficulties of the last few months, survived the doubts and difficulties of a whole lifetime. He felt calm, cleansed—even, plump and battered though he was, beautiful. And if, as he had told himself while walking home, he was getting old, maybe this was the famous serenity of old age. It would be wonderful if it lasted for ever....

And even after he had gotten up, washed his face, had some coffee, and fed Philip, he still felt serene. So serene that he went, wearing a heavy red sweater, onto his terrace, and having merely smiled towards the cold, bright morning and the blue, brilliant sky—smiled at it, welcomed it, and felt happy to see it, but not indulged in any of that nonsense about bringing it to life; of *course* it was alive, whether he was there or not, and would be when he was no longer alive himself—made some decisions. First, he told himself, he would cut down his expenses, whether Betty and Bernard went on helping him or not; it was both humiliating and unnecessary to have to rely on other people all the time, when he was perfectly capable of relying on himself. Then second—which was perhaps a corollary of the first—he decided that he would drastically reduce his social life. For a start he would begin to be a little bit selective about whom he asked, and would not ask someone a second time, just to have an extra person at the table, if he hadn't really liked them the first, and then he would start accepting more invitations himself. In the past he had nearly always refused to go to other people's lunches or dinners, though of course he was asked almost every day, on the theory that the party, not being his, wasn't altogether under his control; couldn't, completely, be orchestrated by him. He was—or was afraid he might be—simply one of the tricks, and not the conjurer himself. But now that too—that infantile egoism, for it was nothing else—would be set aside, and he would accept invitations at least as often as he gave them. What was more, he told himself, he would go and be content just to be one of the guests; and wouldn't, as he sometimes had, try rather grotesquely to monopolize the whole evening.

The third thing he decided was that from now on he would divide his day rigidly into two parts; in the first part doing the translations which would pay the bills, and in the second working on his novel—which would be, apart from anything else, as he had told Bernard, a form of insurance for his old age. And that the novel would be finished, would be good, would be published and successful, he had no doubts at all on this clear, crisp morning....

The last decision that he made as he stood there on his terrace, shining more brightly than the January sun itself, was that he would, in an hour or two, call both Betty and Bernard, and invite them to dinner tomorrow night. And over dinner he would talk to them, tell them everything; and make them both admit that the stories they had told him were nothing but inventions. Oh, it would be grand, he thought, and he should have done it years ago; done it when Pam and Jim were still alive. He should have invited the whole of his inner court, all together, and then—in the nicest possible way of course—presented them with the evidence of their own folly; of the childishness and uselessness of their bickering. He wondered what stories Pam would have told of the others; and Jim ... Perhaps they would never have become real friends—there would have been too much for them to forgive in themselves to make that possible—but they could, at least, have been civil to each other thereafter. And they could, at least, have stopped tormenting themselves.

How he wished he had done it years ago, he told himself as he turned, at last, and went back inside. That he hadn't, of course, had been entirely due to his own selfish motives and pride. But if it was too late to make amends to Pam and Jim—to Betty and Bernard he could, and would; and do it—

in case he had, by some misfortune, any further reason to regret his not having done it—without delay.

He would do it, he thought, as if their lives depended on it. . . .

NINE

Those decisions taken, he spent the whole of that day in a state of euphoria that bordered on self-righteousness. He grinned for no apparent reason, he tapped his foot in tune with a song that came drifting up to him from someone else's radio, he typed away at furious speed and translated forty pages of some really—by the time he had finished with it—enchanting comedy, and he spent what seemed like hours talking to the cat.

'My beautiful old Philip,' he told the sleek and shining animal, 'we have been very wicked recently. We've been frivolous and stupid. We mistook the coincidences and turns of fate for the powers of magic and art.'

For what else had first those blows in August, and then Pam and Jim's deaths right after they had refused him money, been, if not coincidences? And not even particularly surprising coincidences. The blows had all had different causes, if the same effect, and anyway had all fallen from that vacuum at the centre of the year, holiday time, when people were not themselves; and the deaths of his two friends had probably been, either directly or indirectly, a result of some major psychic disturbance of which a refusal to lend him money had been but a small and comprehensible symptom. Pam had been made weak and careless by her impossible fantasy of leaving Rome; and Jim, upset by his relationship with the dreadful Chuck, and hating himself for being involved in such a shabby and squalid situation, had gone out with the intention—if only subconscious intention—of finding someone who would put an end to that squalor for ever.

And what else had all that followed been but the natural

pattern that must have sprung from such tragic events?

'We've been mad and venal,' he told Philip. 'Carrying on with this wretched pretence just because we were frightened of having a few thousand dollars a year less. You'll just have to eat less fillet steak, my beauty, and I shall have to cut down on the scotch.

'Oh Philip,' he said, 'there's going to be order in this house at last.

'Oh Philip,' he said, 'we're going to have peace.'

Peace, and truth, and happiness....

He even felt happy when he phoned Betty and Bernard, asking them to dinner the following night, and he didn't so much as grimace when Betty, after he had told her that Bernard would be there, gasped with an audible shudder and said, her voice soft with the anticipation of forbidden pleasures, 'Oh *Wilbur*'; and didn't so much as flinch when Bernard cried, 'you're going to do it, you marvellous old motherfucker! Tell me what dish you're going to slip the strychnine in, so I can watch her death-throes.'

In fact, the only thing in the whole day that didn't go exactly as planned was the session he had set aside for work on his novel. Because for some reason his head was so full of spring—of buds, and wheeling birds, warm skies and plump white clouds—that he couldn't concentrate on what he was supposed to be doing; and as, after half an hour and only two sentences, this block threatened to introduce just the smallest flat note into the triumphant new symphony of his life, he quit trying. But it would only be for that day, he told himself; and he certainly wasn't about to let this change of plans get him down.

What he did instead was go, for the first time in years, for an aimless, gentle walk through the Sunday city (and so upset and confused had he been of late, and so euphoric today, that he had completely lost track of time, and hadn't realized that today was a Sunday, in spite of the fact that neither Lillian nor Aida had come); an aimless gentle walk under a sky that almost exactly matched the spring he felt within. For though it was only January, and though this morning, early, had been so cold, now, as he wandered through Piazza Navona looking at laughing children holding brightly-coloured balloons, and wandered along the side of the full, rich, flowering Tiber, it seemed like April out, so warm and kind was the air, so full of smells of roasted coffee and baking bread every angle of the streets. And how pleasant people looked, how splendid were the palaces, how grand and glorious the churches. Oh how happy, how happy, how *happy* he was!

He even said 'buongiorno' to four total strangers—a business man type, an old woman, and two gaily-coloured students—and they all smiled and said 'buongiorno' back to him.

That evening, as a start to his new regime of austerity, and though he had only eaten an apple and a sandwich at lunch—eaten as he had sat attempting to work at his novel—he had a quiet and frugal dinner by himself, with only one whisky before, two glasses of wine with his food, and one tiny glass of liqueur afterwards.

It was one of the most satisfying meals he could remember....

Next morning, however, in spite of his having once again slept well, not everything went so smoothly.

For a start, the weather was grey and bitter, with a dampness in the air that penetrated every ill-fitting window and door, and which even the quite efficient central heating seemed incapable of combating.

Then Lillian, when he told her to phone and invite just three people for dinner on Wednesday, and five on Saturday, remembered that while he had been away in Porto Ercole at least six old friends of his from the States, and two more from Paris, had called and said they were in town for a week and were longing to see him.

So he was obliged to invite two of his American friends for dinner on Thursday, the other four for lunch on Friday, and the two French friends for dinner on Friday....

And then again, when he asked Aida, who was a Junoesque girl from the country with two children and no apparent husband, if from now on she could come just three days a week instead of every day, she said it was impossible; she preferred, or rather she had to have, a full time job; and if not with him, then....

But in spite of the weather, and in spite of these setbacks to his schemes for economy, Wilbur refused to become depressed. Yesterday had been exceptional, he told himself, and it was foolish to think that every day would be so very pleasant and rose-coloured. And of course one couldn't just scale down drastically like that, especially if it involved hurting someone as nice as Aida, or being rude to old friends. He would have instead to fade things out, little by little, making a snip here, a snip there, until—maybe only after a month—the garment of his reduced life was the right shape and size.

He didn't even get depressed when, once again, he found it impossible to work on his novel. It wasn't so much today that he couldn't concentrate, he excused himself with, but more that he honestly didn't have time. Because what with talking to Lillian, and discussing with her various ways of saving the odd lira here and there, and having a tearful and upsetting half-hour with Aida—which involved not only assuring her repeatedly that of *course* she could continue to come to him, and of *course* he was delighted with her work, and that not only he, but Philip too, adored her, but also insisting on her lying down for a while to get over her shock, and giving her a brandy, and generally looking after her—it was past eleven before he could sit down at his typewriter and start to work on his translations; and as it was the translations that paid the bills, and as, from now on, the bills had to be paid somehow, and without relying on anyone else....

He translated continuously till two-thirty, as yesterday only having an apple and a sandwich for lunch; and though he did go so far as to clear his table and set out his manuscript, as he looked at the page he was working on he realized that he was too tired to write well. So he put it aside, and went, instead, to have a sleep.

And he *had* to sleep, he thought, if he was going to be on top form tonight. And he had to be on top form tonight....

He slept till five-thirty, and woke both thankful that he had slept, and in the very best of spirits. No, today hadn't been exactly as he had planned it, but this evening, he was both determined and sure, would be. There were going to be no hitches *there*. Everything was going to be perfect; and as he took a quick bath before going into the kitchen to start preparing the dinner, he started smiling as he imagined Betty and Bernard's faces as he sat between them and, instead of playing his usual part, quite seriously told them that for years they had been behaving like idiots, and never so much as in the last few months, but that now was the time to let bygones be bygones, and to start behaving like adults instead. We are all survivors, he would tell them, and it's time we recognized all that we have in common, rather than dwell on what divided us. Oh, he smiled at his plump pink reflection in the mirror, at his round almost cherubic face, he would, for the first time ever, play the part of a wise old man; a father. Of course he would try not to be too pompous, and too sickeningly moral, and of course he would try to say his piece with plenty of jokes and laughs, and without being overly prim; but say it, in one way or another, he would. Even if he did have to be sickening. But there were times when one just had to take a stand; and this was one of them.

'They'll never believe I had it in me,' he told Philip.

He would never have believed it himself.

Betty was the first to arrive, at precisely eight-thirty. And if Wilbur had done a lot today, from the look of it Betty had done even more—though all to herself. She was, as he told her when she swept with the shyest of smiles through the door, dazzling. Her head was wrapped in a black silk scarf, which plunged all the way down her back to the floor, and was dotted with tiny glittering stones that could have been beads but, knowing Betty, were jewels. Her lifted face was as smooth and rapt as the marble Saint Theresa's. Her dress, too, was black, though unembellished except for a diamond and black-pearl clasp. And over her slim white shoulders was slung a black sable cloak that swept in the dust at her feet.

She was already, magnificently, in mourning....

'Come in, my dear,' Wilbur, who was dressed as usual in baggy pants, unironed shirt, and an insufficiently darned yellow sweater, said to her after he had finished complimenting her. 'Come in and have a drink.'

'Oh Wilbur dear,' Betty gasped with a giggle, 'I feel as nervous as I was when I went to my debutante ball.'

'You're quite crazy you know, going out like that. Someone might have bopped you on the head just for an inch of your scarf.'

'I know. But I couldn't resist dressing up tonight.'

'Well I'm afraid we're having a very simple meal, my dear. It's austerity time in George Hall.'

'Nothing you ever do is simple, my love. And tonight of all nights won't be, even if we only eat bread and cheese.'

'It's not that simple,' Wilbur smiled. 'Corn bread and black-eyed peas for us sophisticated folk, and some little crab dish for our Northern friend.'

'Oh *dear* Wilbur,' Betty breathed.

Ten minutes later—ten minutes during which Wilbur and Betty spoke of the weather, a new book that neither had read, and a new film that neither had seen but were both going to just as soon as they possibly could—Bernard arrived. And if Betty had dressed up for the occasion, Bernard had dressed down, clearly thinking that the expected outcome of the evening called for celebration, and not mourning. He wore a Hawaiïan shirt, a vivid check jacket, grubby beige trousers that were too short and showed acid green socks, and a pair of broken down leather bedroom slippers. He carried a greasy looking overcoat in one hand, and a bottle of champagne in the other.

'Am I the last to arrive?' he shouted as he came in, his voice both squeakier and more gruff than Wilbur had ever heard it. 'Betty, are you there?'

'I'm here, Bernard,' the magnolia scented tones floated from the living room.

'Here,' Bernard said, handing Wilbur the champagne. 'That's for later.'

And then, throwing his coat on a table by the door, and followed closely by Wilbur, he strode into the living room and stopped in front of the seated Betty, both of whose hands were raised and ready to be kissed.

'What do you want me to do, bite them or shake them?' Bernard cackled, as he himself sat down without doing either. 'Nice to see you Betty. How are you?'

'Oh, *I'm* very well Bernard,' Betty smiled graciously, as she lowered her hands. '*You*, I see, haven't changed.'

'Now children, behave yourselves,' Wilbur said. 'And Bernard, if you like to fix yourself a drink, I shall go into the kitchen and get us something to nibble on.'

'Nibble,' Bernard snorted.

'Just while we have our drinks. The serious eating comes later.'

'Well thank Christ for that.' Once again Bernard snorted. 'What have you made us? Funeral baked meats?'

'Oh Bernard,' Wilbur said as he left the room, and his fat old friend cackled into his beard.

Normally, Wilbur never served anything with drinks before dinner—unless he didn't have enough food, and was trying to take away everyone's appetite—but tonight he had lavished almost more care on his snacks than on the dinner itself. There was duck pâté and pheasant pâté and a bit of pâté de foie gras. There were celery sticks and nuts, and crackers in the shape of flowers. There were various types of cheese, and canapés of one sort or another. There was even some caviar, that he had found in a jar at the back of a cupboard, and had spread on dry toast. All set in a heavy dish, in the middle of which there was a monkey, playing a mandolin.

He had done all this because it was before dinner, he had decided, that he was going to make his speech; force the signing of the truce. The dinner, afterwards, would be more in the nature of a peace offering.

And five minutes later, make his speech he did. He settled Philip on his lap, by way of moral support, raised his hand, and, having indicated the dish he had prepared, which hadn't been touched so far, so unwilling were both Betty and Bernard to take their whole-hearted attention from each other, said: 'Now listen children, I have to speak to you. And both of you will please listen to your uncle Wilbur in silence, without any comment whatsoever. Because for once in my life I intend to be serious, and I can tell you it isn't easy for me. So—'

How transfigured Betty's face was, as she gently moistened her lips with her tongue; and how hard it was for Bernard to suppress some laugh, or comment, or obscenity....

'Over the last six months, I have lost, in more or less tragic circumstances, two of my oldest friends, both of whom both of *you*—with my active and I must say reprehensible connivance—believe were, let's say, done to death by me. Well, my first point is that of course this pretence, at least on my part, was nothing more than a joke in very poor taste. And I think—and hope—that for both of you it was nothing more than a joke, either. I sincerely hope in fact that neither of you believe I could ever do such a thing—I mean—oh, it's all too absurd, and I'm blushing as I say this.'

He was, too.

'I mean—well, one just doesn't kill people, does one? However, for one reason or another I can't help feeling that this so-called joke has gotten out of control, and over the last few days both of you have told me elaborate stories about each other, neither of which, I'm afraid—or rather glad—to say, I believe a word of.'

He paused for a moment, to give time for that to sink in. But he didn't dare look at either Betty or Bernard, and only heard that, to cover their evident embarrassment, both of them had attacked the food he had prepared for them. Then he went on.

'You also both, still by way of a joke I'm sure, more or less suggested that I should—' he paused again. He couldn't say 'kill'. 'That I should work my magic, let's say, on the other, to avenge the supposed wrongs of the past that both of you consider the other responsible for. Well, all I have to say is this: that I simply—as I said—don't believe in these wrongs, and think that this joke *has* gone far enough, and that both of you—all of us, because I'm just as much to blame—have been behaving in a childish and most unamusing way. And the reason I asked you both here tonight was to say that it's time these illusionary hatchets were buried. Those that divided you from Jim and Pam it is, unfortunately, too late to bury. But for us—oh my dears, let's stop this nonsense.

We're all quite old, and there is quite enough division in the world without us adding *our* portion to it. So now, well of course I don't expect brotherly love to descend like golden rain, but *do* let's all just be a bit more—a bit more—'

But he had finished. And like a gas balloon that has suddenly been punctured, he fell with a flop to the earth.

And then there was silence. A silence that went on and on. A silence of such extreme, such acute embarrassment that he thought, for a moment, that none of them would ever be able to break it, and they would sit like that round the small table until the moth got them, and they dissolved, very slowly, into dust.

It was Betty who eventually—but she was, after all, from the old South, where manners were held to be more important than virtue—broke the immense and all pervading quiet; who shattered the spell that threatened to entomb them for ever. Very gently slipping out a hand and taking a morsel of toast with caviar piled black and shiny on it, and slipping it even more gently into her mouth and down, straight down into her stomach, without any apparent movement of her jaws, she murmured 'Wilbur dear, where *did* you get this caviar? It has the oddest taste, but is *quite* delicious.'

And that did it. The curse was lifted; the statues came to life. Bernard cackled, and said, 'Oh caviar, balls, it's probably just toad spawn, I wouldn't touch it if I were you,' Philip jumped to the floor, stretched, and did a sort of pirouette over an imaginary mouse, and Wilbur himself, with a huge sigh, and a hardly enunciated 'Oh my dears,' said, 'Oh Bernard, it is not. It is just something I've been keeping aside for a special occasion like this. And now let me freshen your drinks.'

And so, he thought, as, the drinks freshened, he went into the kitchen to check what was happening in the oven, he had done it. And while he couldn't help admitting to himself that he was just a little disappointed that neither Betty nor Bernard had said anything, made any sort of statement to the effect that of course they had made those stories up and were ashamed of themselves for having done so, he supposed in the long run their reaction had been quite the most civilized possible; and therefore, probably also the best.

Civilized or not, however, after another half an hour, he couldn't help admitting that he was more than just a little disappointed. He was really most disappointed. Because, as he had thought beforehand, and actually said to them, while of course he didn't expect brotherly love to suddenly rain down on them all, he had hoped his speech might produce —apart from some even nominal confession—something more than the mere chilly drizzle of politeness that now dampened the evening. But they all sat round, waiting for the dinner to be served, being so formal and stiff with each other —Betty as warm as an ice-princess on a day when the temperature is only just above freezing; Bernard, after that first little crack about toad-spawn, as attentive and well behaved as a sycophantic boy-scout—that he wanted to scream. Or at least stand on his head, do a tap dance, or make funny hats for them all.

He tried every trick he knew. He made jokes, he told yet another story about his childhood, he tried to goad Bernard into being foul-mouthed, and he tried to tempt Betty into recounting the story of the affair she had once had with an Eskimo. He positively sweated with the effort to amuse them, even more than he had that dreadful evening before the letter from the tax-department had arrived. But it was all to no avail. Bernard sat grave and portentous, and offered the monkey dish to Betty saying no, he wouldn't eat anything himself, and Betty carefully picked out the caviar-covered toast and observed, every time she did so, that if there was one thing she couldn't resist, it was caviar—and especially this caviar, which was *so* delicious.

And by the time he asked them to come to table, and Bernard asked if they would be so kind as to excuse him for one moment, he had to wash his hands, Wilbur had given up hope altogether. Had given up even trying. Maybe, he thought, he had been too optimistic in expecting them to be cheerful after his little speech. If so—well, it just meant that they weren't going to have a very enjoyable evening. Still, it didn't really matter, he told himself, as he took Betty by the arm and escorted her to the table, and tomorrow they would all be back to normal. And though there was nothing that discouraged him more than a spiritless dinner, he certainly didn't regret having made his speech. On the contrary. And if he had to sit through a hundred spiritless dinners as a result, he would still have made it; and still felt relieved and at peace with himself for having done so.

But it was just at that point—just as he was pulling Betty's chair back for her and lowering her carefully into it, that the tone of the evening suddenly changed. And changed in a way that Wilbur hadn't foreseen, and not at all for the better. Because as Betty sat down, she lifted a swan-like arm towards Wilbur's neck, pulled him down towards her, and, glancing in the direction of the bathroom where Bernard was still washing his hands or doing whatever he was doing, instead of giving Wilbur the kiss he was expecting, whispered with the sweetest smile towards an invisible audience, 'Wilbur, I shall never, ever forgive you. I have never, ever, been so humiliated in my entire life. And while I have no intention of walking out of here in a rage, which would really satisfy that monster—about whom every word I told you is true, every single word, whatever lies *he's* told you—I shall never ever speak to you again. How could you treat me in this way? How could you doubt me? After all I've done for you. No my dear, in spite of all the fun we've had together, there are some things that cannot be forgiven. And this is one of them. My God, I feel as if you're making me *eat* my poor Tommy. And now I shall say no more about it, and will leave after dinner as if nothing had happened. But you will do me the favour of never phoning me or making any attempts to see me in your entire life. And needless to say, there will be no more loans from this particular old sucker. This evening you have shattered my entire faith in life which I believed that you had restored to me after Tommy's death. You have destroyed me, Wilbur. Destroyed me. And now—no more.'

And so saying, and with a gentle push of the swan-like arm, Betty released him, and giving a clear, bright, ringing laugh, a laugh of the most irrepressible enthusiasm, cried to the returning Bernard, 'Bernard, I was just telling Wilbur that he is the most marvellous creature on this earth. Don't you think so?'

'Yes,' Bernard said, with absolutely no enthusiasm, and sat down. 'A true friend.'

How Wilbur walked into the kitchen, brought the first course to the table, served it and begged Betty and Bernard to start eating immediately, without waiting for him—'French politeness my dears, French politeness. Respect for the food'—he didn't know.

Nor did he know how he passed the salt round, kept the wine glasses filled, offered second helpings, cleared the plates away, replaced them with others, and served the second course.

He didn't even know how, while he was doing this, he managed to tell his two guests that they must, simply must come to the opening of a show of paintings by a young painter, a friend of his, whose work was so interesting it couldn't be missed; and how, if they possibly could, they should go down to Catania to hear the first performance of a recently discovered opera by Bellini in which the most charming young soprano, with the freshest, sweetest voice—not one of those awful drag-ass types—was singing the leading role;

and how, if they were free, they should both, yes both of them, together, come to dinner on Friday when he had two French friends coming who were quite wonderful; he was a collector of painted glass, and she, who had a Finnish mother, had ten white cats, all of whom she took with her every summer to an island off the coast of Finland her mother owned, where there was a ruined castle which was incredibly beautiful, and oh how he loved the image of this dear dotty lady with her ten white cats all going for walks together over the rocks under that Finnish summer sun that almost never set or perhaps never did set because he wasn't sure at what latitude the island or Finland itself was and did either of them know, really his geography was so dreadful which was all the fault of the rather erratic education he had received at the hands of—

He didn't know how he did anything for the first half of that dinner, and he never was to know.

Because as he was clearing away the dishes of the second course, something happened to wipe the memory of the effect that Betty's outburst had had on him out of his mind for ever.

And it was that, with only a sudden clutch of hand to neck, a quick, drawn in breath that sounded like a gasp of surprise, and an expression in the eyes first of outrage, then of accusation, and finally of ugly, naked fear—Betty died.

That she had died, and hadn't just fainted, Wilbur was completely certain, even before she very slowly toppled forward and hit her head on the table; and even before the shock really registered on Bernard's face—at which, for some reason, Wilbur instinctively stared, as if hoping to receive from the fat old man some denial of this unbelievable, but incontrovertible turn of events.

Betty had died; Betty was dead.... In this sober new life of his, in this serious new world that he had come to terms with, in this life and world where art and magic were confined only to the written page or the painted canvas, Betty

Bartlett had died. Betty Bartlett had dropped him; had withdrawn her support. And she had died. She was dead.... The words rose in Wilbur's mind, starting as a numbed whisper, and rising to a shriek. And as they rose ever higher and higher, becoming more and more unbearable, and he stared now back and forth between her black robed body and Bernard's face—on which shock at last registered as plainly as a painted sign; for obviously, though the old man had said he wanted Betty's death, and even, possibly, expected it, the actual fact of it was still, well, shattering—Wilbur felt himself falling forward. Falling towards the table. Was he, too, dying?

No, he realized, two minutes later, as he started to recover from his faint, lying in a flabby, unpressed heap half way under the table, and with a pain above his eye where he must have struck himself as he fell. *He* hadn't died. People like him never died. The artists and magicians of the world....

But then, as he lay there, too weak to get up, wondering what Bernard was doing and why he wasn't helping him, and simply repeating to himself over and over again—but in a dull, hopeless voice now, 'Betty is dead, Betty is dead,' he suddenly became conscious of the most extraordinary noise. A high, tearing noise, like paper being ripped, or like the whine of an electric saw slicing through hard wood. A high, choking noise, like the sound of a baby being strangled. A high, ugly, ruthless noise, like—like—like laughter.

And as he pulled himself up, heaved himself, heavily, back into his chair, he saw that indeed the sound was the sound of laughter; and he also saw why his only friend hadn't tried to haul him up. Because Bernard, his old eyes looking quite mad behind his spectacles, his old mouth open and quivering above his thin little beard, was simply staring at Betty's body and trembling, shaking, screaming with the most insane, hysterical mirth.

'Jesus Christ, Wilbur,' he gasped, in a voice unlike any

Wilbur had ever heard him use, 'Jesus Christ, you've actually done it. You made all that great speech, set the whole scene so well I was convinced you were serious, and then—you do it. You've done it. You've actually *killed* her.'

Wilbur closed his eyes. Killed her. Killed her.... But he hadn't. He hadn't touched her. He hadn't done a thing. He had tried to save her from death—from the death of lies and falsehoods in which she lived. He, the great giver and bringer of life, the enchanter and conjuror, had tried to touch her with his wand. He had tried to *save* her. And she had died.

'What was it? Arsenic in the caviar?' Bernard screeched. 'I noticed you didn't touch any, and you know I can't bear the stuff, and Madam was wolfing it down. Jesus Christ! You're insane, Wilbur. Insane.' And off he went again in a high cackle of laughter.

Wearily Wilbur opened his eyes and gazed at the old man as if from a great distance. Poor Bernard, he thought. He was so pale he looked as if he were going to have a heart attack. And quite naturally. The poor old thing must be scared out of his wits. And the fact that he was laughing so hysterically, and talking about killing, was natural, too. People often did in these circumstances.

Even more wearily, Wilbur got up and went round the table and stood behind Bernard. He put his hands on the shaking shoulders.

'You better go home Bernard,' he said softly, soothingly. 'I'll sort this all out. But it'll probably be a long night, and I don't want you staying up and getting tired.'

'Yes,' Bernard murmured obediently, and stood up without taking his eyes off Betty's slumped-over body. 'Yes,' he repeated. Then, shaking his head and seeming to make a great effort to pull himself out of a trance, he turned to Wilbur and said, 'I would love to stay and see how you *do* get out of it though.'

'Come. Come along,' Wilbur urged, and still with his hands on Bernard's shoulders, guided the old man to the door. 'There, take your coat, and get a taxi home. All right?'

'All right,' Bernard croaked—and now Wilbur heard that he was crying.

'I'll call you in the morning. All right?'

'All right,' Bernard croaked, as he allowed himself to be pushed gently through the front door.

But as he went, the old man shook his head again; and awkwardly, confusedly, muttered to the dark landing outside, 'but you know, what I told you about Betty *was* true.'

For the next five minutes Wilbur simply sat at his place at the table, sipping on a whisky and water, and telling himself that he must be calm, he must be calm, he must be calm. But then he decided, or rather realized, that he must do something. He had to. He couldn't just go on sitting here at the table, with Betty sitting dead beside him. Sitting here and sitting here, until morning came, and Lillian and Aida walked through the door....

Softly, he murmured to the cat, who had jumped onto the table, 'Philip dear, leave Aunt Betty alone. She's dead.'

But what was he going to do? What *could* he do?

He knew what he would have liked to do. He would have liked, as they did in the movies, somehow to get Betty back to her own apartment. To get her back, change her clothes, sit her at her kitchen table, and put a toast-crumby plate, a fishy smelling knife, and an open and empty jar of caviar in front of her—as if, spending the evening alone, she had decided to have a snack, and had died.

But it was all very well to do such things in movies. In real life however—it was preposterous, even to think about it. He could just imagine hauling Betty down the great stone staircase of his palazzo, trailing her black sable cloak behind her, and trying not to tread on her scarf. He could just imagine trying to walk her through the street door, and standing with her in the cold until a taxi came by. He could just imagine saying to the driver, 'Could you help me? My friend is a little stiff....'

No. No. It was out of the question.

What was he going to do then? Call an ambulance and say that Betty had collapsed while at the table? Well, yes, that was the obvious, the only thing to do. Except when they did a post-mortem on her, or whatever they did do to discover the cause of death, what would happen? Because surely, as Bernard had suggested, the caviar, that Betty herself had said tasted odd, had been responsible for her death. And it couldn't just be food-poisoning; no food, however off, however villainous, killed that quickly. So it must, actually, have been poisoned. But how? By whom? He had opened the jar himself, only an hour before Betty had arrived. And he was certain that it had been sealed. Had Bernard, then, to give old Wilbur's joke a helping hand, slipped something onto one of those small square pieces of toast? But no. That too was impossible. Apart from the fact that he had hardly left them alone together, Bernard couldn't, couldn't have done such a thing. One didn't kill people. And yet—Betty was dead.

What was more, he told himself, as he sat there staring at the still white shoulders, if by some freak Betty had been poisoned, and even if there was some perfectly natural explanation for the poisoning, there would obviously be a police investigation. And what would the police make of it, however accidental the tragedy appeared to be? Because surely they must know that he had had tea with Pam the day of her fatal fall. And they *did* know that he had been one of the last people to see Jim alive. And now, if Betty was found dead in his apartment—oh, it was dreadful. For whereas the unsuspicious might put the series of deaths down to coincidence, and he himself—though he didn't dare dwell on the matter for the moment—was tempted once again to put them down to some malign and rampant power of magic; of art gone wild and out of control, the police, without doubt, would see them all as part of a diabolical plot. A plot master-minded and—with the possible exception of Jim's death—executed by one person. By him, Wilbur George. What else could they do?

But what could *he* do?

He didn't know; and as, after another twenty minutes had gone by, he still didn't know, he got up and went to the phone and dialled the emergency number.

And as he asked for an ambulance, and gave his address, he told himself that the only thing he had to remember if he was arrested and taken off to prison, was that he must let Lillian know immediately. So she could come round and give Philip his food—and then make sure that he found a good home....

TEN

Of course, he realized next day, after he had been told by the hospital that Betty hadn't died of food-poisoning, or any other sort of poisoning, but had simply had a cerebral thrombosis that had killed her instantly, he had been overly dramatic last night—imagining being arrested, and planning for Philip's future! Still, under the circumstances, his reaction had been more than justified. After all, it had been a terrible shock, and coming on top of everything else that had happened—

The police weren't even informed of Betty's death, and not one of the papers thought a cerebral thrombosis worth wasting a line of print on. Wilbur took it upon himself to inform Betty's children of their mother's decease, and arranged with the American Embassy for the sending of her body to the States for the funeral—which was where the children wanted it to be. A week later one of these children—a pompous lawyer who presumably took after his father, since he had nothing of Betty's brightness and enthusiasm—flew to Rome to see about the disposal of Betty's effects, her apartment in the city and the house in Porto Ercole. Wilbur spoke to him on the phone, and asked him if he needed any help. No, that won't be necessary, the man said bluntly and almost rudely, as if he suspected Wilbur of wanting to get his hands on some of his mother's more valuable possessions. And no, I don't think I care to know, he said, when Wilbur asked him if he wanted to hear the circumstances of Betty's death. He was so very curt in fact that Wilbur somehow couldn't get round to asking, as he had half intended to, about the man's either dead or deranged younger brother....

But ten days later—ten beautiful, sunny winter days—it was all over. Betty was only a memory; another friend to be missed and mourned. And for the world at large her passing had been dramaless; just another shifting of the sands.

For Wilbur, however, who had passed these ten days in a state of almost exalted calm, of organizing this and seeing to that, of phoning here and phoning there—because though the pompous son had refused his offers of help, he seemed to have no idea how much Wilbur was doing and had already done; things took time in Italy—of finding homes for Betty's animals, and another job for her maid; doing, in other words, absolutely everything possible, including drink an enormous amount of alcohol, to keep himself busy, and stop himself thinking, the end of this period of activity marked, as it had to, a return of the sense of unease he had started to feel after Pam's death. That unease that had only left him when he had decided to sober up and be serious; when he had decided that the truth must be known, and had invited Betty and Bernard for dinner....

And as the relief that he had felt on not being arrested for Betty's death—for it was relief more than anything that had sustained him for these ten days—was replaced by a feeling of fear far worse than any law-court could have inspired in him, and as the weather became bleak again, with the skies grey and yellow, he started, at last, to dwell on the nature of, or the reasons for, Betty's death.

Because while every doctor in the world might put her death down to cerebral thrombosis, that, as so much that the world had had an explanation for of late, meant nothing to him. That, once again, was the explanation for the literal minded and the prosaic. But it couldn't satisfy a poet. It couldn't, and didn't, satisfy Wilbur George.

(It couldn't satisfy Bernard Dale, either. 'You old motherfucker,' he had cried when, as soon as he had heard, Wilbur had phoned him to tell him of the doctors' report. 'You genius. You *are* incredible. How did you do it? What wicked brew did you prepare that would leave no trace?')

And now, as he sat alone in his apartment, staring out of the window at the four o'clock sky when he should have been having his siesta, he *had* to come to terms with what had happened; he had to accept his responsibility. And there were no two ways about it—some malign and rampant power of magic, art gone wild and out of control—call it what he would—call it even some intensely destructive waves, of a purely physical nature, emitted by his brain—he *was* responsible for Betty's death. And therefore, in retrospect, for Pam and Jim's deaths too. He had to be. However much he hated the idea, however alien it was, however much he tried to convince himself that it was lunacy to think so. He was a murderer. A murderer *malgré lui*; but—a murderer nevertheless....

It was terrifying. To be so out of control. To be so condemned to doing what he didn't want to do. To kill, whenever a friend of his refused him money.... God, apart from anything else, it was so *vulgar*; so cheap, mundane, unlike him. If his friends had died for destroying some masterpiece he had written, some painting he had done, at least there would have been something aesthetic about it. But for money.... And where would it end, he asked himself. Where could it end? Oh, that was the most terrifying thing of all, and probably, though it had been a subconscious decision, why he hadn't—and he hadn't—spoken to Bernard at all in the last ten days, apart from that once. Of course he could tell himself it was because he had been too busy. But deep down, he knew it was because he had been scared that if Bernard, even in fun, were to say 'all right, that's it', he, the last, and the best of his friends, would drop dead too.

Yes, he muttered out loud; that was why he hadn't spoken to Bernard. And why, what was more, he would try to avoid speaking to him in the future.

For how long though? Could he simply never see him again, for the rest of his life? No, of course not. One didn't just stop seeing friends because—he hesitated. Because one was frightened of killing them....

Yes, one did stop seeing friends for that.

He sat still until six o'clock. And then, finally, he made up his mind. He would go out now and buy provisions for some time. Then he would come home, call Lillian and Aida and tell them to take a week's holiday—a paid holiday, he would make it clear. Then he would unplug the phone, and put an iron bar across his door. And then he would just stay sealed up here, not speaking to anyone, until he had found some way out of this mess. Until he had discovered how to divert this stream that was flooding and destroying his life. Until he learned how to break the pattern that was threatening to set around him, and crush him. He would just stay up here, and think....

Two hours later, he started. With his childhood.

Were the roots of the evil that was entangling him buried there, he wondered. In his much recounted, always different childhood? In that childhood he had spent being handed round from one person to the other, being taken in, thrown out, taken back? In that childhood in which he had been spoiled and then ignored, smothered with affection and then rejected; used as a pawn in a game of adult lust and adult jealousy, of adult greed and adult need. Was that where the trouble lay? In that childhood in which nothing was ever fixed, nothing ever true, where every day he heard different stories of his dead parents, and different stories of his foster parents, until the only reality he had ever been able to hang on to and pull himself up by had been the reality of books and puppets, of movies and vaudeville shows, of pictures and plays and masks?

Possibly, he told himself. But if it was so, wherever in that jumbled mosaic would he find the thread that led to the terrible tree, whose spreading, suffocating fronds were stretching out now, over all these years, and strangling him? However could he tell which, amongst all those scattered, multi-coloured scraps of paper, were the ones he had to follow all the way back in his treasure-hunt; in his hunt for the diseased, contaminated treasure?

He'd never be able to do it. Not now. Now it was too late; the journey was too far. And if there had been street-signs, monuments, which he could have guided himself by, he had torn them down long ago. Torn them down just so he *wouldn't* always be searching for the one, true, undiscoverable home. The past, he had always maintained, existed only in the present. So what was the point now of maintaining that it existed somewhere else; a sort of Disneyland set back there in the bayous of the human heart or brain, that could be wandered round and explored at will?

There was no point at all....

Well then, he asked himself, did the trouble start later? When he was a young poet, and painter, and actor, and novelist, living in New York and producing crazy, funny poems, wild, fantastic paintings, and comic, unclassifiable novels full of magic and mythology; which, for all that they were highly praised at the time, and for all that he tried to inject into them some vision of reality—some shifting, glimmering, unstable reality, but a reality nevertheless—didn't entirely satisfy him; if only because they didn't quite go far enough; weren't quite strong enough to transform the stony, soaring city about him into anything other than a fortress whose foundations were laid in the unquestioning and unquestionable?

Perhaps his presumptuousness had been his sin; perhaps

some undetected falseness in his position....

Or was it later still, the setting up and setting in of this deadly pattern? When, dissatisfied as he was with himself and his work, he had left America and come to Europe, and after wandering for a year, had finally discovered in Italy, and in Rome, the country and city of his dreams? When he had believed he had found at last the one place on earth that corresponded, in almost every respect, to his own particular vision....

For here it had no longer been necessary to distill, to transform, to create. Here all that was necessary was the living itself; to plug oneself in to the current that was here, there, everywhere about one, and to pulsate with it, tremble with it, glow and burn and blaze with it. And here, too, he had found at last people who knew, instinctively, what he was trying to do; who shared, instinctively, his vision. Above all, the other foreigners he met here. The expatriates and exiles like himself; expatriates and exiles of every different nationality, all of whom had discovered, here, the reality they had rejected, or felt themselves excluded from, elsewhere. This reality that was as unsettled as his childhood; as shifting and glimmering as his poems and paintings and novels....

But, he asked himself at last, had he been wrong all this time, for all these last twenty-five years? Had this feeling of having at last united art and life, spirit and body, been just a delusion; a wicked delusion that now he was being punished for? Perhaps, here, cut off from the influences that had, however haphazardly, formed him, instead of living a higher, truer reality, he was really just finding refuge in a state of mind that had no contact with the outside world. Finding refuge from a world in which if he hadn't precisely failed, he hadn't succeeded as he'd wanted to. Perhaps here, far from having found a home, he was permanently, totally exiled in a dream. A dream, what was more, that depended very largely for its survival on extorted or even stolen money. For much as he liked or loved Pam and Jim and Betty and Bernard, and much as he disliked rhetoric of any kind, he had never been able to help thinking that their vast fortunes, dribs and drabs of which had kept him afloat for all these years, were fortunes that *had* been gained, multiplied and maintained by extortion, exploitation and downright robbery; were fortunes whose capital was suffering and misery, slavery and cruelty and horror. Of course, he had tried, in his way, and with those dribs and drabs, to reconvert this inheritance of suffering and misery into some life-giving, life-enhancing currency. But perhaps, he murmured miserably to himself, exhausted now, he hadn't done enough; hadn't been generous enough in the distribution of this coinage he believed himself so good at minting. Or perhaps, simply, no amount of reconversion could ever cleanse the money he had lived on of its blood—and *here* was the secret of the present state of affairs.

Perhaps, perhaps, perhaps ... Perhaps all these explanations were valid; perhaps none of them were. Perhaps he was merely losing his mind.... Oh, he sighed, he didn't know, and it was all so boring and useless. He didn't know and he couldn't know why all that had happened had happened. All he knew was that it had; and that he must try to prevent it doing so again. But *how*? Not only by not seeing Bernard ever again, but also by not seeing anyone ever again? For who could tell if everything would stop even with Bernard? It might, the horror, just go on spreading out in ever widening circles....

So the only thing to do would be to stay locked up in this apartment for ever; cut off from the world until he himself died....

No! Enough! Enough, he shouted at himself, getting up, turning on the lights, and pouring himself a whisky. It was futile going on like this. Absolutely futile. He would, as he had planned, have a week off; but he wouldn't, he couldn't torture himself the whole time. He must try to relax. He *must.* And hope that by the end of the week things would have sorted themselves out.

They didn't, however, and he couldn't relax, and he couldn't stop torturing himself. And if by the end of his seven days of isolation he had managed to do some translating, and quite a lot of writing, he was still just as miserable and confused as he had been at the beginning. He *couldn't* forget what had happened, and he couldn't help but feel responsible for it; and he still didn't know why it had happened, nor how he could prevent it happening again. Furthermore, he was incapable of making a single decision as to his future. What was the use? He had already tried making decisions....

The only thing he did do, in fact, apart from his translations and working on his novel, was write a letter to Bernard—which he slipped out under the cover of a snowy night to mail—asking him if they could please not see each other for a while—at least until the memory of a certain evening was a little more vague—and begging him never, ever, to mention the subject of money again. Never to offer him a loan, a gift, anything. He would be all right by himself. He was determined to be. Please, he wrote to Bernard. *Please.*

It wasn't any use though; because on the very day that Lillian and Aida returned, and so-called normal life started again, Bernard phoned. Wilbur had told Lillian that he wasn't at home to anyone; but the old man screeched so loudly at the gentle Irish girl that Wilbur, standing by her side, heard every word he said.

'Not at home my ass! Of course he's at home. Don't give me any of that shit. Call him immediately.'

With a sign, and a sigh, Wilbur took the receiver.

'You never get any better, do you,' he murmured.

'Well what's this nonsense you've written me,' Bernard bellowed. 'You're losing your fucking mind. Avoid each other! I've no intention of avoiding you. In fact I'm going to come to dinner tonight, whether you like it or not. You'll just have to set an extra chair at the table if you haven't got room for me. And what's more I have even less intention of not giving you any more money. What do you want me to do? Drop dead? Jesus Christ!'

'Oh Bernard.' Wilbur made his usual response, unable, as usual, to keep from smiling. But it was a tired smile. A sad smile ... 'I wish you wouldn't. I honestly don't need it. But of course you can come to dinner if you insist, and there won't be anyone here. I'm cutting right back.'

'Oh my God,' Bernard croaked. 'I can't stand it. But I'll tell you something else. I went to see my lawyer yesterday, and added a codicil to my will. I'm going to take care of you even after I die. Just so you don't make a pact with the devil, and send me to hell.'

'Oh Bernard, you old fool,' Wilbur said—and now couldn't stop a flush coming to his face. But he didn't think it was a flush of pleasure....

'So for God's sake start behaving normally again. And invite some other people to dinner. I haven't met anyone new for ages. And I'm bored. And being bored makes me bad-tempered. Invite some of your bright young artist types. That way I can have an argument. All right?'

'All right,' Wilbur murmured, without even a pretence of a smile.

For just as he hadn't been able to refuse Betty's invitation to the country, he couldn't refuse Bernard now....

He couldn't refuse him a few days later, either, when Bernard invited himself once more.

And after that he started to feel it was his duty to have him over to dinner almost every night; because he had never seen Bernard in such good form and obviously enjoying himself; baiting the young men, being charming to the young women, amusing the middle-aged, and frightening everyone....

But while he did have him over so much—and was obliged, therefore, to spend just as much as ever on his entertaining, every evening became an ordeal for him, and each one worse than the one before. And instead of relaxing after the first few times, he found himself getting more and more tense; waiting, more and more, for something to happen. He became so very tense, that eventually he couldn't even sleep. Which meant that, though he somehow managed to work on his novel, he was too tired to concentrate on doing his translations, which still flowed in relentlessly. And not doing his translations, he was forced to ask, at the beginning of March, for a loan....

'Ha, I knew it wouldn't last,' Bernard crowed. 'How much do you want?'

'If you could spare me five hundred dollars ...'

'I'll bring you a cheque tonight,' the old man laughed. 'I am coming tonight, aren't I?'

'Yes, Bernard, of course you are,' Wilbur said.

He had tears in his eyes....

He couldn't go on, he told himself. He couldn't go on. He was sweating the whole time, drinking the whole time, hardly sleeping at all. He felt sick, he felt exhausted, he felt, for the first time, almost suicidal.

Yet he had to go on. Day after day, night after night, preparing, planning, cooking, inviting—and then being as bright and witty and magical as he had always been. And he was, he knew. It wasn't like those weeks after Pam had died, when his unease had prevented him from playing the perfect host, when his timing had been off, his delivery wrong. Now, oh God, he *had* to be good. He had to be brilliant. And the effort was killing him.

Surely Bernard must see it, he thought. He must realize what he was doing to him. And while, in the past, there had been periods when the old man had been bored and had invited himself to dinner two or three times a week for six months at a stretch—whenever Pam or Jim or Betty hadn't been among the other guests—now, surely, he must know that it was no longer possible to pretend they were still living in those far-off, carefree days. He *had* to be aware that he was destroying him.

Yet if he was, why was he doing it? Bernard didn't hate him, he was sure—he had nothing to hate him for. So if he didn't hate him—why, why, why did he keep on coming?

He tried to take a hold on himself, tell himself that he was over-tired, and that indeed things were just as they had been in the old days—if not better, since now he didn't have to worry about asking for loans, and didn't have to juggle with A who couldn't see B. But it was no use. Things weren't as they were, and he had three deaths on his conscience, and he was terrified of having a fourth. Because of course Bernard seemed to be enjoying himself enormously at the moment, playing the part of the lone survivor. Yet surely there would come a time when he had a reaction, when he realized that this wasn't all a joke. And what would he do then—if not tell Wilbur that he didn't want to see him any more, and certainly wouldn't give him any more money. And if he did that....

Oh why hadn't he agreed to what was in that letter; accepted those proposals?

Or had he feared that he was simply being tested; and if he *had* agreed....

Oh he couldn't go on, he couldn't go on, Wilbur told himself as March passed into a cold, wet April.

And then, at last, two days after Easter, he told himself: he wouldn't go on.

And taking an atlas off one of the shelves, and opening it at a map of the Southern States, he decided that he would leave Rome.

It was the only thing he could do. To leave this city of his dreams. To leave the enchanted land ... He wouldn't go in a panic, abandoning everything, he thought; and he certainly wouldn't go without regrets. But go he definitely would; and as soon as was decently possible.

His mind made up, he felt, in the days that followed, and for the first time in months, almost at peace. So very much so that he not only permitted himself to start imagining a small white house with wrought-iron balconies somewhere in the old quarter of New Orleans, or Savannah, or Mobile—and how it would look, full of his lifetime's collection—but also determined to make one last attempt to establish the truth—so far as he himself knew what it was—before he left.

And to this end, one evening a week later, he invited Bernard to dinner alone.

'Who else is coming?' the old man barked when he came in the door.

'No one, Bernard. It's just you and me tonight.'

'Oh Christ, you want to have a serious talk with me, don't you? I can see it in your face.'

'Yes Bernard, I do.'

'Oh Christ. What have I done to deserve this?'

'Quite a lot Bernard. Quite a lot,' Wilbur smiled—and giving him a drink, sitting him down in a comfortable chair, and ignoring his frequent interruptions, guffaws, sneers and cackles, proceeded to tell him everything that had happened since the morning he had received the letter from the tax-department. He didn't try to exonerate himself from the blame of Pam and Jim and Betty's deaths—'I *know* I'm responsible,' he said—but he did explain that they hadn't died directly at his hands. It had all been done by magic, he said—a magic that he hadn't used consciously, and couldn't, at all, control. 'I feel guilty. I am guilty,' he muttered; 'but what am I to do? What can I do? Well,' he went on, before Bernard, if he had any intention of doing so, could reply, 'I'll tell you. I've decided to leave Rome, and go back to the States. Because—and I know you'll laugh at me for this—I can't help feeling that Rome itself—for me, anyway—is a magic city. It's an invention of my imagination. And if I go away—well, I'll be safe.'

And then he did stop and give Bernard a chance to speak; though for a while his old friend, holding his little white hands together over his hard fat belly, didn't seem about to. But finally—just as Wilbur was about to go on again—he opened his mouth, sniffed, and, his eyes glistening behind his glasses, said: 'You're such an old fool, Wilbur. Really.' And then he laughed. 'Magic my ass! Really you've lost all your sense of humour. Though I guess under the circumstances—' he stopped, stood up, and went to pour himself another drink. And then, standing by the table where the bottles stood, and laying a hand on Philip, who was sleeping in a fruit bowl, he turned, and went on, chuckling to himself, 'Do you think I'm mad? I know you didn't kill them. Jesus Christ. You, kill anyone? For one thing, I wouldn't stand for it. I'm a very moral old bugger when I want to be. And for another—well, you just wouldn't be capable. I must admit, for a second, when Betty died, I had my doubts—but it was only for a second, and just the result of shock. But I was only joking with you, you ninny.'

'Joking,' Wilbur whispered, feeling utterly worn out, and too deflated to think clearly.

'Yes, of course. It was all a big joke. I thought you understood—and were going along with it because it brought in a little bit of cash. But a good joke's always worth paying for, and after all, you've always prided yourself on being the Court Fool, haven't you? Even Fools have to be paid for their services.'

'But those letters and cheques you sent me, after Pam died,' Wilbur mumbled. 'And those promises of cash you all made me if only I would do away with—'

'All whimsy, jokes, fantasies. We're all much too cut off from real life here. It was all a game for us, a dream. And as we have nothing else to believe in, games and dreams are as good as anything else. I dare say we all got a bit carried away, and ended up half believing that we were being serious. But we weren't, really.'

'But Betty, when I told her that evening—the evening she died—she was so angry that she whispered when you went out to the bathroom that she never wanted to see me again.'

'Well, that was just because she had allowed herself to be carried away. She *had* started to believe it. And suddenly being pulled up like that, having all her fun spoiled, was a shock and humiliation for her. Of course she was furious. I tell you Wilbur, we're frivolous old people. Only jokes and fun are important to us.'

'But when they involve *death*?'

'Oh that made it all the better. Because it did enable us to carry on with our joke, to pretend that it was something more.'

'But they *died*,' Wilbur, still dazed, blurted out. 'They *did* die. So it wasn't a joke. And they all died the second they refused to lend me any more money. How do you explain that? No,' he said, shaking his head, 'it wasn't all a joke. It couldn't have been. I did kill them.'

'Oh for Christ's sake,' Bernard snapped, causing Philip to raise his head from the fruit bowl, 'you didn't kill them. They killed themselves. Don't you understand what I'm saying, you old idiot? Here we are, cut off, living this ridiculous boring life of ours that we haven't got the strength or the energy to change, and with hardly a single point of contact with the outside world—the real world, if you like to call it that. I bet you, even if Pam and Betty and Jim ever read the newspapers, it was only like reading a novel for them. A daily serial. I know it is for me, anyway. Even the stock page in the *Herald Tribune*. They're all just fairy figures, that can't possibly touch us. We were all way beyond that. Nothing could touch us. *Nothing*. Not inflation, nor depressions, nor unemployment—not even a world war. We'd just have packed up if necessary, and moved on, and shifted our funds wherever they'd be safe, wherever they'd go on growing and growing and growing, wherever they'd be on the winning side. In fact, almost the only contact we had with the real world was through you, for all your nonsense. Even though you probably never realized it, you were almost the only outlet we had to—well, life. You *invented* life and the world for us. That's what Fools and so-called artists exist for. You were almost the only thing that kept us, just, tied to sanity. Otherwise we'd all have died, one way or another, years ago. And that's why, when Pam and Jim and Madam Bartlett did decide to cut you off, they were cutting off their life-line, severing their main artery—or their only artery. So of course they died. They had nothing left to keep them going, either spiritually or physically. There now. So let's have no more of your vanity. You've never killed a soul in your life. And I doubt that you ever could.'

But still Wilbur wasn't satisfied. 'But just to tell the *truth* to Betty,' he repeated.

'She didn't *want* the truth,' Bernard screeched. 'It was enough for them—for us,' he corrected himself, 'to believe that you knew it. But they didn't want to hear it. Why do you think we've all stopped you writing for all these years? We didn't give you money so you could write or paint, as you claimed you wanted to. We gave you money just so you *wouldn't*. You were our life-line all right, but we didn't want you to be strong enough to haul us back to dry land. Just to keep us afloat, just *something* to hang onto with the promise of safety if we *did* ever want to be pulled ashore. Now for Christ's sake stop this, and get into the kitchen and do some cooking.'

As if in a trance, Wilbur stood up, and started shuffling across the floor, staring at his feet in their old white sandals. But before he left the room he paused, and said 'But I'm still going to leave Rome. I'm still going away.'

'Over my dead body,' Bernard cackled. 'Over my dead body. Where'll I go to dinner if you leave? Who'll keep me amused? You can't leave Rome. I forbid it.'

'Oh Bernard,' Wilbur sighed—and went.

He should, he thought, as he ate his dinner and tried to chat to Bernard about this and that, be feeling relieved. And perhaps he was. But there was still something that nagged him—still something that kept the lump of unease, though it had been almost cut out, aching in his brain. There was still one last thing to be settled before he could lean back, and acquit himself, and tell himself that this story was, at last, over. Only, dazed as he was, in a trance as he was, he couldn't put his finger on it, and even started to suspect, by the time they had finished eating, that maybe he was imagining things, and had so gotten used to that feeling of unease that he was unwilling, now, to relinquish it.

Then, just as Bernard pulled back from the table and said he should be going, it came to him, the final question he wanted to ask; the final hurdle that stood between him and total peace.

'That story you told me about Betty, and her son, and Arthur—that wasn't true, was it?' he asked.

'Of course it was,' Bernard said, looking irritated. 'Do you think I'm a liar?'

'No, of course not.'

'Well then.'

'But if your story was true, Betty's—'

'Was a lie.'

'Oh,' Wilbur said—and wondered, wearily, if that, at last, had done it.

ELEVEN

That it hadn't—though he had already suspected as much—he didn't discover definitely till next morning.

He had asked Lillian to take an old suitcase out of the bottom of a closet, and start packing a few of his more precious books. (Because he was still determined, whatever Bernard thought, to leave Rome.) The girl had just started, when she called out to him in his study that there was the manuscript of an old novel in the suitcase, and did he want to see it.

'Yes, dear child. Bring it to me. Is it mine?'

'Yes,' Lillian said. 'Didn't you know?'

'No,' Wilbur said; and started, casually, to glance at it. But after he had read the first page of this book he hardly remembered having written, and couldn't at all remember the story of—it had never been published—he became far less casual; and by the time he had read the second, and then the third and fourth, he started to tremble. And by the time he had finished....

The novel was in four interlocking and inter-echoing parts, and was called *Four Children*. The first part told of a widowed English woman who, in order to keep her daughter for herself, does everything possible to prevent her from marrying, until the man the girl loves and is loved by—and she herself cares for—is so confused by the web of lies that the mother, with the aid of two evil acquaintances, weaves about him, that he eventually flees; causing, naturally enough, the total alienation of mother and daughter. The second told of a young and shy student (one of the evil acquaintances of the first story, in earlier years), whose wealthy but weak-minded mother is persuaded by an intelligent, over-bearing, but impoverished girl, who is determined to catch a rich husband, that her twenty-year-old son should be 'brought out', and therefore sends him off on a sort of Grand Tour with this girl as an escort; which ends with the young man humiliated and lonely, having had the girl's schemes revealed to him by a—the—meddling English widow and a cruel and bullying man, falling in love with—and of course being rejected by—the cruel bully. The third part told of a Southern lady (the pushy girl of Part Two, who *had* found her rich husband—who had conveniently dropped dead almost immediately, whereupon she had married again, and had children) whose youngest son, after a traumatic experience with a prostitute, and various dramas with a 45-year-old already retired businessman of sinister reputation, (the shy student, of course) goes mad and gets murdered. And the last part told—as it had to—of a gruff huntin' and fishin' type (the disappointed lover of part one, and the cruel bully) who discovers *his* youngest son, whom he has always wished will grow up to be, unlike himself, an artist, dressed as a confederate soldier and being fed cocaine by a woman he knows (other evil acquaintance of Part One, pushy girl of Part Two, etc.); with the result that the boy, after he has been saved from drug addiction, turns into everything his father *hadn't* wished him to be; a dull and dutiful citizen who goes to church every Sunday with his wife and children, and is not only not an artist, but is not even keen on huntin' and fishin'....

What could it all mean, Wilbur asked himself as he put the manuscript down. What *could* it mean? That—though he didn't remember having done so—he had some time in the long distant past, struck by the similarities between his four main characters and his four best friends (there had been differences, however; the English widow had been small and dark, the Southern lady very beautiful with tiny white teeth, the shy student painfully thin, and the cruel hunter and fisher completely without humour) lent them his novel; and they had so appropriated the stories he had woven about them, finding them far more entertaining than the truth, and justifying their petty dislike of each other, that they had finished by believing what they'd read *was* the truth? Or that he had, extraordinarily, magician that he was, written the truth—with one or two errors in detail—years before he had met either Pam or Jim or Betty or Bernard? Which was why, ironically, when Betty and Bernard had told them their stories, he hadn't at all believed them.... Oh, he didn't know, he didn't know at all. What he did know was that he found, somehow, both theories almost equally frightening; that he had been right to suspect that his lump of unease, in spite of Bernard's explanations last night, hadn't been completely eradicated; and finally that, and now without a moment's delay, he must leave Rome; leave within a month if he could, or even within a week. Leave before it was too late....

TWELVE

He and Lillian and Aida spent the next four days in a state of hysteria. Packing cases were brought and laden with books. Boxes of every shape and size were procured and stuffed with ornaments and treasures. Paintings were taken down and removed from their stretchers. Piles of old clothes were sent to a refugee relief organization. Plants and flowers were given to friends. Enquiries were made as to the cost of putting furniture in storage. Letters were written to the landlord and the telephone company and the electricity company. Cards were sent out—bright little yellow cards; five hundred of them for a start—to places all over the world, announcing that Wilbur George was leaving Rome, and would get in touch with his friends just as soon as he had an address where he could be contacted. Day and night they worked, the three of them, Aida bursting into tears every now and then, and not at all calmed by the fact that Wilbur promised her a whole year's salary in lieu of proper notice, along with whatever severance pay she was entitled to by law.

'But where will I find someone else like you, Signor Wilbur,' she wailed; and Wilbur couldn't even try to tell her.

However, at the end of four days it was almost all done. Everything that was going to be sent was packed and ready; everything that was going to be given away and hadn't been collected was labelled and set aside. The only things that hadn't been done in fact were these: first, no destination had been decided on for the packing cases and boxes that were to be sent; second, no actual arrangements had been made for their sending, nor for the storing of the furniture; third, no tickets had been bought; for either Wilbur or Philip; and fourth, and finally, no money had been obtained, or even asked for by Wilbur, that would enable these last, and unfinished details, to be settled. And without money....

He did his accounts once, twice, three times. He sent Lillian round to all the various film offices who owed him for translations. He estimated the maximum possible amount he might get for his furniture, if he sold it rather than stored it. He even went through his paintings to see if there were any he'd be able to sell immediately.

But it was hopeless. With the best will in the world, and looking on the very brightest of sides, all the conceivable funds he could lay his hands on still wouldn't even cover the year's salary he had promised to Aida, let alone what he owed to Lillian, and would have to pay the removal men, shipping companies and storage people.

And so, he realized, as he sat in the ruins of his wonderland, there was nothing for it; he would have to ask, for one last time, for a loan. And quite a large loan. At least ten thousand dollars. And who else could he possibly ask but Bernard....

Except that Bernard, whom he hadn't seen during these four hectic days—putting him off with stories of not being well, of having to go out himself, of having to finish a particular translation—didn't want him to leave....

It was all so ridiculous, he told himself as he got up now and paced, alone—Lillian and Aida had finally gone home—through the jumbled, disordered, carpetless rooms, stooping every now and then to pick up a feather from the floor, or a broken bead, or to trace a pattern in some gold dust that had spilled. To be so near, to be so absolutely ready for flight; to be sitting in the plane with the doors closed; and then to be told, 'We're sorry, but we haven't any fuel....'

He *had* to leave, he moaned to Philip, who, with all the

turmoil, was almost more distraught than himself, and spent the whole time walking up and down, making funny little croaks and squeaks, and spraying all the packing cases. He *had* to—if only because having, with such insane speed, destroyed the home that it had taken him so long to create, he couldn't, now, even if he'd wanted to, put it together again. It was gone, the magic land, for ever. For not only were the actual trappings all torn down, but the spirit itself of the place had been dismantled. And without the spirit....

At seven o'clock he called Bernard, and asking him if he was free, told him to come over.

'I've been so busy I can't cook,' he said. 'But we can have a drink here, and then go out somewhere.'

Surely, he thought, after he had hung up, Bernard, even though he didn't want him to leave, when he saw just what had been accomplished in four days—saw the disaster—would realize he was serious, and agree that perhaps departure was the best course. Surely he would, he told himself miserably as he managed to free two chairs and set them down in the middle of the chaos with a whisky bottle and two glasses on the bare wooden floor between them. Surely he would....

But he didn't. He seemed, in fact, when he arrived, his little turned down mouth falling open with astonishment—and it was the first time Wilbur had ever seen him like this—truly furious. And there was no twinkle in the eye, no just concealed smile on the lips, when he snarled, 'You've gone out of your head. You're going through your menopause. You're—you're fucking *mad*!'

Wilbur couldn't even say, 'Oh Bernard.'

'Put it back. Put it back this instant,' the old man shouted. 'If you think I'm going to sit in the middle of a store room and have a scotch, you're wrong. You're out of your mind. I should have known you were up to no good, being so busy for the last few days. You've never been *that* busy.'

'Oh Bernard, *do* sit down,' Wilbur managed to get out at last.

'No I will not! I'm too old to start camping out. Now go and put some shoes on and let's go out to a restaurant.'

'No,' Wilbur said, flatly and sulkily. 'I've *got* to talk to you.'

'Well I don't want to talk to you. Not about this, anyway.'

'Bernard, I have to leave. Don't you realize. I mean apart from everything that's happened. My life in Rome is over now. My time's up. I've *got* to go.'

'Well my time isn't up, and you're not going.'

'But *why*, Bernard? We can see each other in the States, I shall probably come back here on a visit at least once a year, and you do know lots of other people here. I'm not your entire social life.'

'Oh fuck your social life. And mine. Of course I know lots of people here, even if most of them are idiots. But do you think I give one damn about that? I don't even give a shit if I never see you again. It's just that I cannot stand hysteria and stupidity, real stupidity, and especially not in you, who I've always thought was the one person in the world who wasn't stupid. I don't give a damn if you go, but you're not going, because I refuse to allow people to make fools of themselves, above all you. I'm doing what everyone's supposed to do, stand by their friends, and you'll be grateful in six months time that I did stop you going. And besides,' he said, his voice lowered a little at last, and finally sitting down with a crash in one of the two chairs Wilbur had set out, 'It's not true that I don't give a damn if you go. Of course I do. At my time of life—or at any time of life—one has to be grateful if one knows *one* sane person. And if you are so lucky, you have to hang on to them. But don't push me,' he added, in case his last statement had seemed too much like an apology, 'because even though I do believe in standing by my friends, and tolerating the odd moment of insanity even in the sane, I won't stand for it for long. I'm not that charitable.'

'Oh Bernard,' Wilbur said, risking a smile, 'no one's ever accused you of being charitable.'

'Just as well too,' the old man huffed, leaning forward and pouring himself a whisky.

'Nevertheless,' Wilbur went on after a while, 'I'm serious.'

But this, just as he was settling down, was too much for Bernard. And beside himself once again, leaping to his feet, and half dropping and half throwing his glass on the floor, he howled, 'Oh *Christ*!' Then he bellowed, 'You are *not* serious Wilbur George, and you never have been and you never will be, and if you were you could never have been a friend of mine because I'm a corrupted bloated disgusting old man whose only talents in life have ever been slaughtering animals, making underhand and extremely profitable deals and seducing preferably poor and defenceless virgins. Therefore do not repeat that word in my presence, and now you have ruined my evening and before you ruin our entire friendship I am going to go and have dinner by myself and get roaring drunk and good night. Good *night*!'

'Good night, Bernard,' Wilbur murmured as the old man stormed out—and for a second, even now, felt a smile coming to his lips. But then he sat down, and poured himself a scotch, and gave in, totally, to despair.

He sat there till one o'clock in the morning; and then, feeling bits of broken glass through his socks, but not caring, went to his bed; the only raft left intact amidst the sea of his life.

He was in despair when he woke next morning, and muttered to Philip, 'we will leave, my beauty', and he spent the whole of that day (he had told Lillian and Aida that there was no point in their coming in) in despair. At least, until six o'clock. And then, at six o'clock, when the bell rang and he opened the door once again to Bernard, he started to feel more cheerful.

Because he saw, immediately, that the old man, having made his scene yesterday, was in quite a different mood today; a mood that promised, at last, well. Rosy cheeked, and dressed in his loudest, most ill-fitting clothes, he came stomping into the apartment, not seeming to notice the shambles about him; and waving an old service revolver in his hand—a service revolver that Wilbur had seen him wave at other times; and always when he was feeling particularly benevolent—he said, 'Still planning on leaving, are you? Well, maybe you aren't so mad. So many fucking communists out demonstrating this afternoon about something that I thought I'd better come out armed.'

'Oh Bernard, you old fool,' Wilbur instinctively said, hoping he didn't sound too relieved at this change for the better. 'It's not loaded, is it?'

''Course it is. What the hell's the use of an unloaded revolver if you're attacked by a mob.'

'I don't think anyone's about to attack you.'

''Course they are. They can smell me. I give out a particular smell that they recognize and distrust instantly. Soap,' he cackled. 'Dirty unwashed lot.'

'Well put it down and come in.'

'Can't imagine why. What's there to come in to? We might just as well stay here.'

'Oh Bernard,' Wilbur said.

'Actually, I'm on my way to the doctor's. But I thought I'd just stop by and make sure you're not crying your eyes out. You *are* still planning on leaving, are you?'

'Yes,' Wilbur said, faintly nervously.

'And if you leave you'll need some money to leave with, right?'

'Oh—er—well—'

'What does that mean?'

'Yes,' Wilbur mumbled. 'But it would only be a loan,' he went on hurriedly. 'A real loan. And just as soon as I get settled I'll start to pay you back.'

'Ha,' Bernard snorted. 'Well, I can't stop now, but come for dinner tomorrow night, and let me know how much you want, and when you want it, and we'll discuss things. All right? It won't be a great meal, because Pino's mother's sick and he's gone away for a week. Fucking servants. But I'll manage to make something, because obviously we can't eat here. All right?'

'All right,' Wilbur said, hardly able to believe how complete this change in Bernard's attitude was.

'Good,' the old man barked. 'See you tomorrow then.'

'Eight-thirty?'

'Eight-thirty.'

And with that, and a sudden, unexpected, and strangely private laugh—a laugh that made Wilbur, for a second, nervous again; made him suspect, for a second, that Bernard was teasing him, playing a game with him—the old man turned, and, stuffing his revolver into the pocket of his jacket, left.

It was wonderful! It was too good to be true! After this hellish day, now, suddenly, everything was transformed! And transformed so quickly that Wilbur felt his breath taken away. He was dizzy, with all the ups and downs. One moment in hell, the next in heaven. And Bernard wasn't playing a game with him, he was sure, in spite of that peculiar laugh he had given. No, of course he wasn't, Wilbur told Philip. He had probably laughed at the memory of the scene yesterday, and at how he had behaved. And now—Oh, he said to the bare patched walls, that all at once seemed more beautiful to him than they had when picture covered—I'm safe. *Safe.*

'We're leaving, Philip,' he told the cat. 'We're leaving.'

'We're leaving,' he told the cat, who was lying on the bed with him, when he awoke in the middle of the night. 'And Uncle Bernard isn't playing a game with us. We really are leaving.'

But as he started to fall asleep again, he couldn't help feeling slightly apprehensive once more. Not because of Bernard's laugh—that had just been a passing incident—nor even because, the excitement and upset of the move apart, it really was an enormous step he was taking, leaving Rome after all these years; leaving the one place he had always believed was home. No, he told himself, he would be able to cope with that. What made him apprehensive was a renewed remembrance of that youthful novel of his, and the impression—the absurd impression, maybe, but the undeniable impression, nevertheless—that until that matter was cleared up, until he did learn the truth, then he *wouldn't* be completely safe. He might not even be able to leave, however much Bernard helped him.

'Oh, we must learn the truth,' he whispered to Philip. 'We must, we must, we *must*.'

He did, in a way, that very next evening. But not in the way he'd been expecting; and not at all in a satisfactory way.

He arrived at Bernard's on the dot of eight-thirty, wearing, for the first time, the new clothes he had bought for himself in Paris, and feeling rather as he imagined a young Victorian man must have felt when going to dinner with his stern and venerable father.

And Bernard, at the beginning of the evening at least, as he let Wilbur in and gave him a drink, behaved like a stern and venerable Victorian father. He seemed, in contrast with his cheerfulness yesterday, and his explosive bad temper of the day before, preoccupied, and slightly absent. He didn't swear, he didn't shout; he didn't even laugh. He just pottered about, straightening the odd silver framed photograph on his dark tables and desks, checking and rechecking that the candles on the dining table were firmly set in their silver holders, asking more than once if Wilbur's drink was all right—'you're sure you don't want any more ice?'—and being generally so unlike his normal self that Wilbur couldn't help asking him, after half an hour had gone by, if he was all right.

'Yes, of course I am, thank you,' Bernard said with a slight frown.

And then, just like that, the mood passed.

'Jesus Christ,' the old man barked, 'I'm getting old. I've been spending the whole day thinking about the past, and having regrets about what I haven't done and what I have done.'

'Oh Bernard....'

'Well, you wait. It'll hit you too, one day. When you suddenly realize that not only has your body gone to pieces, but your brain's gone soft too. Now let's go to the table, and talk about business. Or do you want to eat first?'

'Oh, let's finish our meal in peace,' Wilbur said; wanting to be sure that Bernard's good humour was really firmly established before they did discuss business. Because though he was sure it was going to be all right, if anything went wrong now—oh, he couldn't bear to think about it. No. Tonight had to be the decisive night, and nothing, nothing could go wrong. And then tomorrow, or in a few days—

'You just want to make sure I'm in a good mood, don't you?'

'Yes, of course.'

'Well you needn't worry. I am. In fact,' Bernard growled, 'I'm feeling in a better mood than I have for years.' And then, just as he had when leaving yesterday, he gave that strange, private laugh....

They ate and drank, in spite of Pino's absence, magnificently; and by the time they were through Wilbur was feeling so flushed with contentment, so glowing with wine and candle-light and old china, and had so forgotten that they did have to talk about business, that he was very shortly going to leave, and that he had felt apprehensive when he had woken last night, and much of today too, he was quite shocked when Bernard, wiping the last traces of cream off his lips and beard, said, 'Well, how much do you want, you fugitive?'

'Oh,' Wilbur said. 'Bernard.' And then, recovering himself, and knowing that this was no time for hesitation, added 'Ten thousand dollars.'

Bernard nodded, and sniffed. 'Yes,' he muttered. 'That's about the figure I arrived at, too. And tell me, where are you planning to go?'

'For a start I thought I'd go back to the South somewhere. New Orleans, probably. And then look around from there.'

'Uh-hu,' Bernard muttered. 'And what are you planning to do when you arrive?'

'Well first, obviously, find somewhere to live. And then find some little job that won't take up too much of my time—I don't know, teaching—something like that. But then mainly just writing again seriously for the first time in years.'

Bernard, abandoning his thoughtfulness for a second, cackled. 'I told you. You're not serious.'

'Well I'm going to be from now on,' Wilbur said. 'You just see. I told you,' he murmured, 'I've been working on a new novel for the last few months.'

'Um,' Bernard said, pushing back from the table, and indicating the living room. 'I've been thinking today. And not only about the past.'

'Yes,' Wilbur said, eagerly, as he followed the old man back into the living room and sank down into a deep leather chair.

'And while I apologize for having shouted at you the other night—'

'Yes,' Wilbur said, much less eagerly now, and staring with a renewed flush of apprehension at Bernard, who was still standing, and had his back turned, and was examining something on a table in the corner of the room.

'I've decided that after all—'

'Yes,' Wilbur said, his apprehension turning into terror as he heard the tone, and felt the drift of Bernard's words.

'I can't let you go.'

And so saying, the fat old man turned and faced Wilbur; with the most benign and mischievous expression that Wilbur had ever seen.

It was so benign and mischievous that his first reaction was that Bernard was, once again, teasing him; only pretending to refuse him what he asked. But then it went on being so benign and mischievous, that even as he started to break out in a sweat of relief, he realized that Bernard wasn't teasing him at all, and that his mischievousness was due to the fact that he was enjoying watching the effect his words caused. Which made him, confused and lost, think he was going to pass out.

'Please Bernard,' he gasped. 'Don't tease me. Not now. I've been too tired recently. Perhaps I'm losing my sense of humour. But please just tell me—'

'I did just tell you,' the old man chortled, and started advancing towards Wilbur, his little turned down mouth glistening, his eyes dancing with lights. And then, as he advanced, Wilbur saw what he had been examining on the table, and now he carried in his hands. In one, there was a sheet of paper; and in the other, his old service revolver....

'I'm not going to let you go,' Bernard said, his voice horribly quiet and sneering. 'Why should I? I've been paying for you for all these years to play the fool, to dance when I snapped my fingers, to amuse me and humiliate yourself—why should I stop now, now that I'm old and alone?'

And still he advanced, as Wilbur pressed himself back in his chair; trying to retreat from this horror, this obscenity; from this whispered, jeering evil....

'You must be crazy. Oh of course, I've never minded giving you a little bit of cash so you could entertain me, but if you think I'm going to give you ten thousand dollars so you can go to New Orleans and set up house there and amuse other people—you're mistaken, Wilbur George. It's just a matter of economics. As I say, I don't mind paying for my entertainment, but I'm not going to invest in a failure.'

He was right on top of him now, leaning over him, his hideous little words being spat in Wilbur's face, his hideous little hands clutching the revolver just an inch from Wilbur's heart ... And as he went on, went on and on, spewing out this poison, Wilbur felt his eyes fill with tears, and Bernard's loathsome form, looming over him, became blurred. He started to shake his head, whimpering 'Stop it Bernard. Stop it.'

But Bernard wouldn't stop it.

'And that's what you are, isn't it?' he hissed. 'Or would be, if I let you go. A failure. A flabby, pathetic failure. Because you daren't go on, do you? You daren't go all the way. You don't have the guts. You've created this whole world here for yourself, and always kidded yourself that it's all just tinsel and make believe. But now that you see it's the real thing, that it's the *only* thing—you want to run away. Run back to the ready-made, the second-hand, the cast-off.'

'Stop it Bernard,' Wilbur sobbed. 'Please, please stop it.'

'No, I won't stop it,' the cruel old bully spat. 'Here, take

this,' he said, thrusting the revolver into Wilbur's hand. 'Hang on to that. Perhaps that'll make you feel more courageous. Another magic wand to wave. Ha,' he laughed, 'you wizard. You *artist* you. You're all the same. You don't mind crawling on your bellies in front of a whole lot of bored, useless people to beg for their petty cash—as long as you can despise them and feel superior to them. And as long as you can kid yourself that you're free, and that you can go on entertaining them for as long as it suits you. But the second someone points out that you depend on them, that you're not free, or even worse, threatens to cut off your funds—you howl and blubber and want to run home to mother.'

He had to stop it! He couldn't go on listening to this filth. He was falling backwards into space; back through a space full of lies and unspeakable horrors. 'Stop it stop it stop it,' he started to chant hysterically. 'Stop it stop it stop it.'

'Don't worry though. I *will* keep on giving you hand-outs. Only by God you're going to have to earn them. Every day from now on you're going to have to play for me, you puppet—'

'Stop it stop it stop it—'

'And you'll never leave Rome, never. You'll go on with a red rubber nose stuck on your face and laugh and perform as you're pelted with rotten apples, and you'll eat shit, all the shit in the world, and you'll swear it tastes like nectar, and you'll be my lackey, my servant, my slave. And I'll live to be a hundred years old, and even when your liver's given out and you're crippled I'll still drag you from your bed and make you dance for me, grovel for me, lie for me. And I'll never free you, and I'll never give you the money to leave. Never, never, *never*!'

And finally Wilbur could take it no more. He *had* to stop it. And raising the magic wand that Bernard had thrust into his hand, and holding it against the huge hard belly looming over him, crushing him, he squeezed it....

He didn't know which was more shattering; the bang, or the silence that followed. The silence that was only broken by the slow, soft bump of Bernard crumpling backwards onto the floor, the whole of his old yellow shirt stained and splattered with blood....

Wilbur didn't move for almost a minute; simply staring at the smoking gun in his hand, and telling himself that he had killed someone. He had killed someone ... And not by magic now. Now he had actually killed someone; actually, materially, murdered someone. He had taken a human life....

But after a minute, though he was still too utterly stunned to know exactly what he was doing, he stood up; stood up and stared, now, at Bernard's bleeding, shattered body. He stared at it not to see better the crime he had committed; but because that body, lying on the floor, was shaking. And it wasn't—yet—shaking with death throes, nor even with pain. It was shaking—with laughter....

And after he had stared at it for another few seconds, Wilbur suddenly, sickeningly, and without the slightest doubt, knew what the dying old man was laughing about.

'Bernard,' he whispered, his voice no more than the thinnest thread in that dark, gloomy room, 'you did it on purpose.'

'Well of course I did,' his old friend cackled—with surprising strength. 'Of *course* I did you ninny.'

'Oh Bernard ...'

'But stop wasting time. Get a handkerchief and wipe your fingerprints off the gun and give it to me.'

It was a dream. An awful dream. A nightmare....

'Go on, do what I say. Quickly.'

Slowly, in a dream, Wilbur did it; and Bernard took the gun in his right hand.

'As a matter of fact,' the old man gasped, 'I thought you might kill me right out. So I left instructions here for you, and an explanation.' He indicated, with a twitch, the sheet of paper in his other hand. 'Now take this, take it home and burn it.'

In a dream, Wilbur stooped, and removed the sheet of paper from the little white hand, and put it in his pocket.

'Now get out of here. And make sure no one sees you leaving. Go and tell everyone you spent the evening at home.' Again, though agonizingly now, and with a dribble of blood from the corners of his little turned down mouth, Bernard cackled. 'I've left a suicide note on the desk in my study. And as the doctor told me yesterday—though I knew it anyway—that I had a very serious heart condition, everyone'll think that I had one last magnificent dinner with a friend—they need never know who, if you keep your mouth shut—and then decided not to wait for mother nature to do her work. I always was an impatient old bugger.'

'But *why*?' Wilbur moaned, beginning at last, however terrifyingly, to see some logic in the nightmare.

'Why do you think?' Bernard cackled, even more bloodily. 'It was all just a joke. You always had this great thing about making art and life one. And when I refused you money—you killed me. So now they really are one. And now you'll *never* be able to separate them again. It was all,' he repeated, 'just a joke.'

'Oh Bernard ...'

'Now get out of here.'

'You don't want me to wait?'

'Good God no. And anyway, it won't be long now. It's starting to hurt like hell.'

'But I can't just—'

'Oh get *out*,' Bernard hissed.

And so, slowly, Wilbur bent over and kissed his old dying friend—who whispered, with a final cackle, 'I told you I'd taken care of you in my will'—and then, even more slowly, started, with only one backward glance, to leave the room. And then to leave the apartment. And he was almost at the door before he heard Bernard, very weakly, call, 'Wilbur?'

'Yes, you old fool,' he called softly back.

'Take care.'

What more?

Two months later—two months which he spent just camping out in his apartment, writing and waiting for Bernard's extremely generous legacy to come through—Wilbur, having put everything he possessed into storage, left Rome. He didn't know precisely where he was going—having chosen a cargo boat that left Naples and made lots of different stops, all round the world; including, eventually, Naples again—nor did he really care. He simply—left. With a small suitcase in one hand, Philip in a cat-basket in another, the now almost completed manuscript of his novel in a shoulder bag—and oh, it *was* going to be good; he'd *really* done it this time; he'd *really* gone all the way—and an unease as cold and heavy as a head-stone in his heart.

But though he did feel this unease, and knew, now, that it would never leave him, he didn't—and this was perhaps the one thing that ensured it would never leave him—altogether regret it. Because in spite of all the events of the last year, in spite, even, of the fact that he was a murderer, he couldn't help feeling and being aware that his life—and therefore his art—was, as a result, immeasurably richer. In fact, he told himself, his unease was only a sort of tax he would henceforth have to pay; a tax on the value that had been added to his life....

And so saying, he set sail; only adding, as his small black ship moved out into the glorious, polluted, summer-blue bay of Naples, that since this story had started with a tax on added value, it was highly suitable that on this note it should end.

HUGH FLEETWOOD was born and educated in England. At the age of 21 he went to Italy, where he has lived for most of the past twelve years. Until his first book was published he taught English in Rome; since then he has supported himself by his writing, and painting. He has written seven novels, for one of which—*The Girl Who Passed For Normal*—he was awarded the John Llewellyn Rhys Memorial Prize for 1974.